Waiting for No One

a sequel to Wild Orchid

D1550475

Red Deer PRESS

MAY   2012

Published by Red Deer Press, A Fitzhenry & Whiteside Company
195 Allstate Parkway, Markham, ON L3R 4T8
www.reddeerpress.com

Published in the United States by Red Deer Press, A Fitzhenry & Whiteside Company
311 Washington Street, Brighton, Massachusetts 02135

Edited by Peter Carver
Cover and text design by Tanya Montini
Cover image courtesy GettyImages & Veer
Printed and bound in Canada by Webcom

5 4 3 2

We acknowledge with thanks the Canada Council for the Arts, and the Ontario Arts Council for their support of our publishing program. We acknowledge the financial support of the Government of Canada through the Canada Book Fund (CBF) for our publishing activities.

 Canada Council for the Arts Conseil des Arts du Canada  ONTARIO ARTS COUNCIL CONSEIL DES ARTS DE L'ONTARIO

Library and Archives Canada Cataloguing in Publication
Brenna, Beverley A.
Waiting for no one / Beverley Brenna.
ISBN 978-0-88995-437-3
1. Asperger's syndrome—Juvenile fiction. I. Title.
PS8553.R382W33 2010   jC813'.54   C2010-904510-6

Publisher Cataloging-in-Publication Data (U.S.)
Brenna, Beverley.
Waiting for no one / Beverley Brenna.
[256] p. : cm.
ISBN: 978-0-88995-437-3 (pbk.)
1. Asperger's syndrome – Juvenile fiction. I. Title.
[Fic] dc22 PZ7.B74663Wa 2010

ANCIENT FOREST™ FRIENDLY

21 trees were saved for our forests

Preserving our environment

Red Deer Press chose to print the pages of this book on recycled paper and saved these resources[1]:

	energy	water	greenhouse gases	solid waste
	9 million BTUs	35,945 L	956 kg	273 kg

Printed by **Webcom Inc.** on Legacy Hi-Bulk Natural 100% post-consumer waste.

98%

FSC
www.fsc.org
MIX
Paper from responsible sources
FSC® C004071

[1]Estimates were made using the Environmental Defense Paper Calculator.

For Snowflake, a cat who was particularly astute and who taught me that pets can support people in many ways.

Chapter One

THE JOB INTERVIEW

"What qualifies you for this position?" she asks, at 10:30 AM, on Friday, October 4. I do my best to look at her, but I can't quite meet her eyes. Looking people in the eyes is not one of my skills. I try and think of an answer, but it's difficult because I don't actually understand the question. I hear swear words in my head but I restrain them there. I know it would be extremely unintelligent to use swear words during a job interview, and this interview is very, very important to me.

"Um, do you have any ... any water?" I stammer as politely as I can. This is one of the things I have learned from reading plays by Harold Pinter. Sometimes you can respond to a question with another question.

"Certainly. Just a moment," she says. She is obviously well practiced in answering politely. Her mouth snaps shut in a straight line. It looks like a red subtraction sign. She gets up and goes over to the corner where there is a Culligan water jug, and I notice that from the back she resembles Danny DeVito, one of my favorite actors. I especially admire his performance in the movie *Throw Momma from the Train*, in which his character plots to kill his mother. I can certainly identify with this, but I would never murder my mother, because that is against the law, even if she gets on my nerves.

Danny DeVito has an amazing ability to act as if he is out of control, and I identify with this, as well. The difference, of course, is that when I am out of control, I am not acting. It's all real.

The manager of this bookstore does not look as if she has ever been out of control in her life. When she turns to face me, she looks more like the Queen than Danny DeVito. Every hair is in place. So unlike the way I think I look. I stare at her mouth and hear another swear word repeating itself in my brain. I'd really like to go for a long walk right now, but that's not a smart idea if you're having a job interview.

After handing me a cup of water, the manager sits back down in her chair. I hope she has forgotten her question. She has.

"So, tell me about your previous job at the bookstore in Waskesiu. What was the bookstore like? What were your duties?" Her mouth widens and I think she is smiling. Or

Beverley Brenna

possibly just stretching her lips. There should be a manual for this. *Mouth Codes*, it would be called. *Correctly match the mouth to the emotion and be socially astute.*

I am quiet for a minute. It gets confusing when people ask you more than one question at a time, especially if they are smiling when they do it, because then you have to think about their emotions along with the actual questions. Right now, one part of my brain is thinking of things like, "The bookstore at Waskesiu is in a log building by the lake. Its interior smells like resin and pine needles. The windows are small and it stays unusually cool inside." Meanwhile, another part of my brain is thinking of things like, "I looked at people when they came into the store. I asked if I could help them. When they paid for things, I put their money into the cash register and gave them their change." While I am thinking these things, another part of my brain is hanging onto the swear words.

Because I am thinking of so many things, I can't get a message to my mouth to tell it exactly what to say. So instead of answering her questions, I blurt out: "I like gerbils." I have already warned myself not to initiate a conversation about gerbils during this interview, and now I have done it anyway. Sometimes, against the judgment of the smart part of my brain, I just can't help myself.

I have been looking for a job in a bookstore because

I have a bookstore reference and I can tell the setting would be comfortable for me, but I can tell this interview is not going well. Things have not turned out the way I planned. At the very beginning, I tried to control the way everything would go—the résumé, the application, the job interview. But what's happening now just goes to show that life is unpredictable. Sometimes things don't go according to plan.

When I wrote my résumé, I gave careful thought to the models my high school teacher provided us last year and, in the end, I was proud of the result. My mother— who ended up in her bedroom having a temper tantrum because I did not do the résumé her way—was not proud of the result. She was certain that I would never be hired for this or any job. She was convinced that, although I have the skills required to work in a bookstore, nobody will want me because I made two errors while doing my résumé. The first error, in her opinion, was that I printed the résumé on blue paper, which she thought made it look unprofessional; I thought using blue was superior because blue is a more advanced form of white. The second error, according to my mother, was that I used my new gerbil as one of my references.

"Taylor Jane, you cannot use a gerbil as a reference," she told me, but anyone could see that I had already done it.

Beverley Brenna

I'd put his name down in the space under *Mrs. Thomson, Manager of Waskesiu Books,* and *Mrs. Thomson, English Teacher.* It bothers me that the Thomson names are the same, even though they are really two different people, but I'm getting used to it. At least they have different phone numbers. When I first put their two names on the résumé, though, it bothered me so much that I started thinking of gerbils as I always do when I'm getting upset, and Harold Pinter's name just sort of fell onto the page. Harold Pinter: gerbil. Not Harold Pinter: playwright. I wish I knew Harold Pinter the playwright, but I do not. He lives in England and I have never been there.

After I'd written down my gerbil's name, I liked the way it looked. I thought that anyone reading the résumé would be interested to see a name like Harold Pinter on it and eventually they might ask a leading question, which could result in my telling them about gerbils without initiating the topic. I know that initiating conversations about gerbils is not always appropriate. If asked, I planned to indicate that I like gerbils, and to confide that I included Harold Pinter's name because he is my gerbil and I take very smart care of him. I could then discuss why I named him Harold Pinter—because I greatly admire the plays of Harold Pinter, which is an important fact if the person considering me for a job is looking for someone who likes literature. And this is the purpose of having a résumé in the first place: to teach people about yourself.

The rest of my résumé teaches other things about me. Under *Strengths* I have listed seven, and the first one I included was *smart organizer*. Then I put *truthful*, because that would always be advantageous in an employee, and *manages time well*. I deliberated before I added *independent* because it's only recently that I have begun to think of myself as independent. But better late than never, and so I put it down. And then I put, *has Asperger's Syndrome*. I thought hard about that one, too, because some of it is a strength and some of it isn't. But most characteristics could be either smart or bad, depending on the situation. So I left it in.

My other strengths are: *smart at writing, likes books,* and *strong-willed*. That last one could be part of my Asperger's Syndrome, but then again, it might be separate. It could actually be a negative thing, like if my employer wanted me to do something I didn't want to do and I'd say, "No way, I'm not doing that!" But if a customer was trying to break the rules, as in trying to stuff a book into a big black knapsack without paying for it, I would speak out, and this is where *strong-willed* would be positive. In the end, I didn't put down *strong-willed*, but I planned to explain all this to the person if I got an interview.

Beverley Brenna

When I was in high school, Mrs. Thomson the English teacher told me that sometimes it helps to write down your feelings. I kept a journal over the summer, and Mrs. Thomson was right. It did help me understand things better. Now I have a new computer—a Toshiba—which I got from the university to help me complete my biology class. Instead of keeping a journal on this laptop, in addition to using it for my class, I am writing a book. It is a book about me. When you consider all the books in the world, you might think that another one is not needed. But that would be incorrect. The world can always use another book because there are so many different perspectives that can be shared, and every person's perspective is important. Including mine: Taylor Jane Simon, age eighteen and three-quarters, would-be bookstore employee.

When I was finishing my résumé, I added: *trying to quit swearing*—but then I figured that this would be confiding that I haven't been successful yet, so I took it out. It is not lying to leave things out. It is just being careful, if you really want the job, and I do. Also, without putting anything down about swearing, I had seven things under *Strengths* and seven always feels like the right number ... although, I am trying to get over that. Numbers should not be associated with feelings because numbers are inanimate and not to be confused with the animal kingdom, nor do they take part in the chemical language of nature.

The place where I brought my résumé is the Eighth Street Bookstore. I have been in here before, looking for books. When I was a lot younger, I didn't read much, because I was afraid of what might be in anything new. The only book I'd look at was *Alexander and the Terrible Horrible No Good Very Bad Day* by Judith Viorst, because my parents had read it to me so often that I had it memorized and nothing in it was a surprise. I also memorized *Charlotte's Web*, which my parents read aloud nineteen times. Now I know that if I am reading something for the first time, and I don't like a part, I can just skip over that part or close the book. Knowing this means I am in control. Once you realize you are in control of a situation, you will be all right.

What I really wish right now is that I could control job interviews the same way I control books. If this were possible, I would skip over this job interview. I would go from the part where I delivered the résumé, to the phone call telling me that I either did, or did not, get the job. But real life isn't like that. You can't skip the bad parts, because if you did, you'd be skipping all the other parts, too. And then you'd have nothing.

Chapter Two

MORE OF THE BAD PARTS

When I went to deliver my résumé this morning, I got to the store at 10:26 AM. Instead of simply dropping it off, however, I dropped it off *and* I got to talk to the manager. That was where the bad parts began. If I had just dropped off the résumé and gone home, I would have had a job interview another time, and today could have been a predictable day.

Instead, when I tried to hand the résumé to a person at a desk, the person said I should talk to the manager. Then the person stood up and led me to where the manager was. When I handed the manager the envelope, she said, "Oh, Mrs. Thomson phoned me about you. Can you stay for an interview?"

I said, "I am not dressed appropriately."

But she said, "Oh, yes, you look just fine." So that was the way I got the interview so fast.

I think she was incorrect in her evaluation of my

clothing because I know that for an interview you are supposed to wear a skirt and blouse, a matching jacket if you have one, panty hose, and shoes with heels. I do not like wearing panty hose, but I was going to buy some for the interview. Panty hose remind me of Teflon, and the idea of having Teflon on my legs is repugnant because Teflon is only for frying pans. And it causes cancer.

Instead of wearing an appropriate interview outfit, I had put on my jean dress, because I like the way it feels, and my running shoes. On my head I was wearing a woven cap—blue, the same color as my eyes, and people say it makes me look very modern and stylish. When I wear it, my long black hair hangs out from under it, but not over my face. I can't stand anything touching my face.

The manager led me to an office and I sat down in a chair. She told me to sit in another chair, by the table, and I suddenly noticed that I had taken a seat at her desk. That was probably a mistake. You shouldn't go into someone's office and sit at their work station. Possibly she was concerned about germs or DNA and she would have to spray things down after I left. That is what I would do if someone came into my room and touched my things. I didn't touch her computer, though. I know about that.

I sat at the table and she sat across from me. She

took my résumé out of the envelope and looked at it. Then she said, "Is it okay if I ask you a few questions?" I told her that I haven't had a chance to study anything, but she said that would be fine. This was when she asked me the qualifying question, "What qualifies you for this position?" Because I didn't understand this question, I began to get anxious, and after her next two questions came out together, my thoughts got all mixed up. That's when I introduced the topic of gerbils.

I hadn't meant to talk about gerbils so soon, and only if she asked me after seeing Harold Pinter's name on the résumé. Damn, I thought. Goddamn questions, now they've got me all worked up.

"And do you know that the CIA used gerbils in airports due to their ability to smell the sweat on people and identify them as potential criminals because of the heightened adrenalin?" I finish.

"Oh, yes. Well. I've heard they make nice pets," she says, and then there is a silence. I can tell she is not interested in gerbils. Or in major crime investigations in airports.

"I have a brand new gerbil," I say. "Gerbillus perpallidus." I have a sudden urge to clean the table between us with the sleeve of my dress, but I don't give in.

"Oh, that must be nice," she says. I can tell she is not

Waiting for No One

11

thinking that it would be nice to have a gerbil, because she is looking at her watch. People look at their watches when they are bored or are thinking about going away and doing something else.

"What is your name?" I ask, taking over the asking questions role.

"Marian Timmons," she says. "I'm sorry, I should have introduced myself earlier."

Now, the name Timmons is a little too close to Thomson. I don't like names that are similar. I have a hard time distinguishing them. As soon as she says, "Timmons," her name gets pushed out of my head by "Thomson."

"Mrs. Thomson?" I ask. Goddamn names! I know her name isn't Mrs. Thomson. I feel like such an idiot.

"No, Mrs. Timmons," she corrects.

"That's what I meant," I say. "Mrs. Thomson. Timmons. It's very nice to meet you. Your front reminds me of Helen Mirren in *The Queen*." I probably shouldn't have said that because you're not supposed to talk about people's fronts. But this woman has hair exactly like Helen Mirren in her portrayal of Queen Elizabeth, and her smile looks like a minus sign. Anyway, it is probably better to say who she looks like from the front, rather than who she looks like from the rear, which is Danny DeVito. I have already discovered that most females do not want to look like Danny DeVito. I go on, speaking very quickly in the breathless way I do when I'm not comfortable.

"As you can see by my résumé, I have lots of strengths that I displayed in my last and only job at the Waskesiu bookstore. I showed 'smart organization' in the way I took things out of boxes and put them on the shelves. I showed 'truthfulness' by giving people the exact change. I showed 'manages time well' by always being on time for work except for once when I was late. But that didn't count because I'd been lost and you can't be on time when you're lost. I showed 'independence' because I actually got the job without my mother's help. I am a smart writer and I like books. Especially plays. And, in addition, I have Asperger's Syndrome, which potentially makes me strong-willed, as you will see if anyone here breaks the rules and I have to confront them, but possibly I got strong-willed just from my personality. Or my mother. She is strong-willed as well."

I wish that I hadn't mentioned my mother. You are not supposed to talk about your mother in a job interview.

Mrs. Timmons stretches her lips even wider when I am finished. They look like slices of red pepper.

"You have done an admirable job of putting down your strengths," she says. "Many people find this hard to do."

I should just leave it at that. But there is a silence in the conversation and I feel as if it is up to me to fill it, as if silence were an empty glass and I was holding a pitcher of water.

"I thought of one other thing," I say, all the while inside my head saying *Shut up. Shut up!* "At first I put down, *trying to quit swearing*," I go on against my smart will, "and then I took it off. I thought it might be a negative thing to include."

"Oh," she says. "Well."

"Shit," I say.

Mrs. Timmons' mouth makes a shape like a whole red pepper, only eighty-five percent smaller. I go on.

"I mean, I didn't mean to say that! Any of that, including—including the swear at the end," I stammer. "I know that using swears is not the best demonstration of one's vocabulary, goddamn it." And I am frankly aware that in interviews you're supposed to keep your volume at a two or a three out of ten, and now I could hear that my voice was at least an eight and definitely in the red zone.

"Yes," she says. "Well." Now she resembles Danny DeVito from the front as well as the back. Then she stands up. "Let's have a look at the bookstore, shall we? And you can see what the people do who are on counter shifts."

Counter shifts. Although I know it is silly, I picture

Beverley Brenna

people wearing math counters instead of dresses. *Shifts of counters*. I can't help chuckling and then I blurt out, "Goddamn it, shut up," but Mrs. Timmons is ahead of me and maybe she doesn't hear. I dislike it when people laugh and do not explain what they are laughing at, but in this case, I think she has not heard me.

We go to the middle of the store where there is a long lineup of people waiting beside a rope. As if they are cattle in a corral. The front people go up to a big desk where three cashiers are helping them. These employees must have the counter shifts, I think, because they are taking turns counting the money.

The lineup is confusing because the cashiers do not know which person will end up at their till. I can tell that if I am one of the cashiers, this will bother me. I will look at the waiting people, and I will not be able to predict which customer I'll end up with. Then, once a customer comes to me, I will have to make change, while at the same time guessing which person will be next. This gives me the shivers.

I think this lineup must bother the customers, as well. It would even bother cattle to be in a lineup like this. I have heard that cows like to know where they are going as much as people do.

"I do not like the lineup," I say to Mrs. Timmons.

"Well, it's busier than usual right now," she says. "Usually it's not this bad. Or good, depending on how you look at it. We certainly like the business, that's for sure!"

I am still looking at all the people. They are waiting quietly now, but what if they start talking? It could get pretty loud in here. One thing I do not like is loudness in public places. Then I notice that two of the people are wearing yellow. I do not like yellow. I try not to look at them but I look anyway. Then I sneeze. Twice.

"Bless you," says Mrs. Timmons.

Even thinking about yellow makes me sneeze, and I am thinking about it now. I sneeze again, luckily swallowing another *Shit* before it comes out. I do not think this interview is going well at all.

We go back to her office and I sit down. "Tell me about the books you like," says Mrs. Timmons. It is a relief to be back in the office, away from all the people who wear yellow and might get loud. I tell her about *Charlotte's Web*, and the way my parents read it to me over and over. Then I talk about the books I read in high school, and especially about *The Catcher in the Rye* by J.D. Salinger.

"And you mentioned that you like to read plays," she says.

"Yes," I say. "I started with *The Birthday Party* by

Beverley Brenna

16

Harold Pinter the playwright. Most recently I have enjoyed *Waiting for Godot*. I saw it as a noon show in the drama department at the university. Then I read it. I like the way Samuel Beckett's characters can't remember anybody's name right."

"I see," says Mrs. Timmons. She rubs her eyes and I wonder if she is actually having trouble seeing, and saying the opposite of that, which is something people often do—say the opposite of the truth—but I will never know. Since the name issue is only one thing I like about Samuel Beckett's play, I go on.

"Through the whole play, these two characters, named Vladimir and Estragon, are standing under a tree, waiting for someone. They are very confused about what they are doing there and feel ridiculous in their whole beings, but there is one thing encouraging them and that is hope. The play is not really about two people under a tree. It is about the experience of life. And waiting. And feeling ridiculous. And hope."

"I see," she says, again.

"But there is some swearing in it," I say, "and that's bad."

There is another silence.

"In the program I got at the theater," I go on, "it said that the play was performed at San Quentin prison and the inmates liked it. Probably because they understand what it's like to be tied down." The manager still doesn't say anything, so I continue. "The play reminds me of real life," I say. "We are fastened here, having a conversation. This is our experience. But I am waiting for it to be over. And feeling ridiculous because I am not wearing appropriate clothes. And, at the same time, trying to be hopeful."

When I look up, Mrs. Timmons is looking at me.

"Have you read any other plays?" she asks. She is not rubbing her eyes any longer. "Well, yes," I say. "I have read other plays by Harold Pinter the playwright."

"And which plays of Harold Pinter's have you read?"

"All of them," I say.

"All of them?" she asks, her eyebrows raised. I think she is looking surprised. I am not sure why.

"I think so," I say. "Unless he's written something new and I haven't seen it yet."

"And what do you like about Pinter's plays?"

"Nothing is certain," I say. "That's the point in a lot of them. The uncertainty of everything. It makes me feel calmer to know that other people share my sense of waiting on the edge of a precipice, knowing the danger but trying not to think about it. You can't see what's ahead; you just know the ground is falling away in front of you. One wrong step and you're over. So you just wait there."

"Hmm," says Mrs. Timmons. "That's very interesting."

"And you will have no harness," I say. "Which you would have if you were an actual mountain climber. But life is not like mountain climbing. It is even more unpredictable, and in life, there is a lot of waiting instead of going up and down hills."

Mrs. Timmons is looking at me strangely. She has an expression I cannot identify. It's not a bad one, I think, but I don't know if it's a positive one, either.

"There are a lot of swear words in these plays," I say. "In case you wanted to know."

"You indicate you are taking a university class," Mrs. Timmons says, finally, looking back at my résumé. "I am guessing it's philosophy?"

"Biology," I answer. I suddenly realize she has been asking all the questions. I should try to balance things.

"Have you ever taken a biology class?" I ask.

"No," she says. And then we just look at each other.

All of a sudden, the interview is over. Mrs. Timmons shakes my hand and says she'll call me and let me know her decision. I want to take my résumé back, but she's already put it away in her desk, so I just say, "Thank you for the interview," and leave the bookstore. I am proud of the way I closed the conversation, and at least this part of the interview—the ending—is just the way it should have been.

So now I am waiting. I am waiting by the phone. I could be baking cookies, but I feel too jumpy to measure things properly. I feel like cleaning things and then cleaning over what I have already cleaned. This is not a happy feeling and I am looking for a way to make it stop.

I keep thinking of all those strangers, lined up with their books. Wearing yellow. Getting loud. Maybe this job is not for me. I spent seven hours writing my résumé and thirty-two minutes having the interview, and now there is nothing to show for it, which is an equation that doesn't balance. If I don't get this job, I don't know what other kind of job I could get. Quite possibly I will get no job at all. Which makes the final result zero.

All sorts of words are rushing through my brain. People with no jobs have no money and limited independence, which is what my mother is always warning me about. If I do not get a job, I will not be independent and I will never move away from home. If I never move away from home, I will always be living with my mother, unless one of us dies, which is expected to happen but not for a long time. If I don't get this job, I will be living with my mother for about forty more years.

Maybe she was right. Right about the blue paper and using my gerbil's name. That's what makes me the maddest about this whole event. That maybe, in this situation, my mother was right, after all, when she distributed her advice. But as long as the manager hasn't called me, and I haven't heard I am not getting the job, I might be getting the job. So for now, it is just like Vladimir and Estragon, waiting under the tree, holding on to one thing, and that's hope.

Chapter Three

HAROLD PINTER

At 11:25 AM, twenty-three minutes after the job interview is over, I decide that when Mrs. Timmons calls, I will say that I am actually not interested in a job at the bookstore after all. I will say that my university class might take up more time than I had initially thought, and that I might need all my extra time for studying. I will be very careful not to swear when I say this. My university class isn't the only reason I have for not taking the job, but it isn't lying if you leave things out of an explanation.

Two minutes after I make this decision, I start to make the cookies, but I am not concentrating because of the swear words I can hear in my head. I end up burning the cookies, and then I realize I left out the eggs. The eggs are still sitting on the shelf where I placed them, right beside the pan of blackened and flat baking. I try to scrape the cookies off the cookie sheet and realize they are stuck there because the cookie sheet is not made of Teflon. This makes me think about panty hose. Even though I hate wearing panty hose, I should have worn some at the interview. Four minutes later, I realize that things are not as bad as they seemed at first, because I saved the eggs.

The eggs were a Safeway special at one carton for a dollar. This means that each egg cost less than nine cents. Actually, each egg cost 8.3 cents with a repeating decimal, which is not possible in real life because if the cost of something has a repeating decimal, it would take forever to pay. Math and life are not the same thing. I wish they were, because then life, like math, would be totally predictable. But life is something without a repeating decimal and this is what I am trying to get used to.

I wash all the dishes and then I go to see Harold Pinter. He is in his cage at the bottom of the stairs, and when he hears me coming, he stirs up the little nest of shavings he's made for himself in an old toilet paper tube.

"Hey, Harold Pinter," I say, tapping the top of the cage, but very gently, so as not to disturb him too much. "So there you are again."

In my mind, I'm replaying some of the first lines from *Waiting for Godot*. After I say, "So there you are again," Harold Pinter is supposed to say, "Am I?" as if he were the character named Estragon. And then I say, as Vladimir, "I'm glad to see you back. I thought you were gone forever." Then he'll say, "Me too." And I say, "Together again at last! We'll have to celebrate this!"

This is the joyous part about waiting when there are two of you. At least you can share the bad times.

"I have to go soon," I say quietly, knowing that Harold Pinter will not answer me. "I promise I will come back," I add.

I remember that when I was little, I was always afraid that someone who went away would never come back. I can remember feeling terrible every time my father went to work, because even though he had always come home before, I couldn't predict that he would come home this time. After all, each day is different—something I have had to get used to—but some things will stay the same. Like a person going to work and then coming home again.

Of course, when my father went to Cody, Wyoming, he didn't come back. So maybe I was right to be anxious. I have been able to go there and visit him, not always successfully, and I am supposed to be going there again for Thanksgiving.

"I promise I will come back," I say again to Harold Pinter, careful not to scare him. I talk softly because gerbils are nocturnal and I don't want to disturb him in his sleepy state.

I know he won't answer me, but I prefer talking to him as if he could. As if maybe someday he'll rise up on

Beverley Brenna

his back legs, sniff the air, and then offer a reply. Stranger things have happened in this world.

I reach my hand into the cage and, with one finger inside the tube, carefully stroke his back. I can feel the tiny bones under his fur. It is amazing to me that bones this delicate can hold him together.

"I messed up again," I tell him. He blinks and trembles as if he is afraid, but I know it's just his way of purring, and, through his skin, I can feel his little heart beating.

"I don't think I'm going to get that job," I say. "I'm waiting for Mrs. Timmons to call but I don't think she's going to offer me the job. And even if she does, I'm probably not going to accept it. Or maybe I am. I haven't decided." I blink back tears. It isn't mature to cry when you're eighteen and three-quarters. "I'm waiting for her to call and, while I'm waiting, I'm trying to pick which of the two opposite words I will say: *yes*, or *no*. Unless she doesn't offer me the job at all, and then I will just have to say thank you and hang up without swearing."

Harold Pinter goes back to sleep and I begin to see that my dilemma is not that important. It's not a life or death matter. It's only a job. I decide to postpone thinking about it, which is possible with any problem, unless you're in a life or death situation, and I go upstairs. Mom is in the kitchen, making lunch. It is one of her EDOS: earned days off. She has been sleeping in late and her cheeks look flushed. Her eyes look puffy, too.

"Taylor, did you drop off your application this morning?" she asks.

"Yes," I say, and close my mouth tightly. There is no need to tell her everything.

"Did you get to talk to anyone?" she goes on, stirring something into the macaroni that looks like blood and gore.

"I talked to the manager," I say. The name Mrs. Thomson flashes into my head, but I know that's not right. I squeeze my hands together and then begin to dig my thumbs into the opposite palms.

"What's her name?" my mother asks, as I knew she would.

"Never mind," I say. "It's private."

"It is not private," says my mom. "She's the manager of a bookstore, for heaven's sake. I could call there right now and ask who the manager is, and someone would tell me. So it's not any big secret."

"I don't remember," I say. "It's something like Thomson but it isn't that."

"Taylor, don't be impossible," she says. Now that makes me start to feel mad, and at the same time, I can feel my IQ dropping as it always does when my emotions get the better of me.

Beverley Brenna

"What did she say?" my mother asks.

"A lot of things. Too many to tell you because I'm going to have lunch and then go to my biology class. Remember, it's Friday, and I have classes Mondays, Wednesdays, and Fridays. And a lab on Tuesday and Thursday mornings." I am practically bouncing up and down I'm trying so hard to control myself. There is so much I could tell her about the interview but I want desperately to remember it alone, because as soon as my mother is allowed to know about it, she will stick her own perspective on top of mine and that just gets confusing.

"Will she call you back about an interview?" asks my mom. Penelope Simon is the kind of person who just never gives up. Sometimes I am kind of like her, but sometimes I'm not.

"I don't know," I say. "I already had one interview, but it's possible I'll get another." Damn! Right away I wish I hadn't told her.

"You had the interview?" Mom asks. "This morning?"

"Yes," I say, going to the fridge and pulling out some old pancakes left over from breakfast. I pick one up and chew it cold, trying to eat fast so I won't talk.

"Stop and listen to me, Taylor," says Mom. "So you had the job interview this morning! How did it go?"

Now that's the kind of question that always makes

me mad. *How did it go?* What exactly does that mean? *How* is one of those words that I skip over, and then I try to figure out the meaning of the rest of the sentence. In this case, *go* is the verb, used to describe movement. As far as I know, the interview never went anywhere.

"Nowhere!" I said.

"What?" asks Mom, the macaroni spoon dripping its red juices.

"It went nowhere, and I probably won't get the job, and even if I do, I don't want it," I say. "Now I have to go, as in the correct usage of the verb, or I'll be late for class. I have to go to class, and then I'll come back for dinner and go to bed, and then, tomorrow, which is Saturday, I will clean my closet and sort things into boxes, and then on Sunday I will have church, and then after church I will have the ballroom dancing class, which I am beginning not to like because it is too competitive a sport for me."

"But—" Mom calls after me, except I am already gone. Out the door, onto my bike, and heading toward the university, as if I could leave the situation in the kitchen completely behind me. Which I can't. The memory of Mom standing by the stove, with that disgusting spoon, won't erase itself from my head. And on her face is this expression I have learned means "disappointed." She is disappointed. By me. As if it's not enough that I am disappointing myself.

Chapter Four

TRYING TO TAKE MY MIND OFF THINGS

I bought Harold Pinter five days ago on Sunday, September 29, at 2 PM, at the Ace Pet Store in Market Mall. He is only two months old but he already knows the right way to poke the latch of the cage until it opens. He has escaped three times, but each time I found him right away. To keep him from escaping again, I keep a book on top of the cage. The book that is there now is called *The Care and Keeping of You*. It is the healthy body book that my mom bought me when I was eleven. I don't need it anymore, although sometimes I like to look at the pictures, just to remind myself that personal hygiene is important. Bathing has never been a preferred activity for me, as the truth of the matter is: water hurts.

For the first three days, I kept my biology textbook on top of the cage instead of *The Care and Keeping of You*, because the textbook was the heaviest book I could think of and I knew it would keep Harold Pinter secure.

Then I realized that I need to read the textbook for my biology class, so, two days ago, I decided not to keep it on top of the cage. This was smart thinking because there is a unit exam coming up and our professor says we should do a lot of review reading, so I am going to, even though I have a photographic memory for what I read, especially if it's to do with biology.

The textbook is called Biology: *Concepts and Connections* and it has 783 pages, not including the tables, answers to chapter quizzes, glossary, and index. Including the supplementary pages, the total page count is exactly 1,110 pages. Some of the pages at the end of the book are not numbered, which is very annoying, and I had to count them myself.

When I went to the Ace Pet Store, I wasn't sure if I'd feel comfortable, seeing another gerbil after Hammy died, but once I made up my mind to go and look, I felt confident that looking, at least, was the right thing to do. Hammy was my last gerbil, and before that I had Charlotte, and before her, I had June, and before her, I had Walnut, and he was the first gerbil I ever had.

Walnut was a Mongolian gerbil, and my dad bought him for me. Mom and Dad had been yelling at each other, as they often did when we all lived together in the same house, and then Dad asked if I wanted to go for a drive.

We drove for twenty-five minutes, just looking at things. Then we drove by a pet store two times, and, on the third time past, we stopped and went in. I asked for a cat. My dad said no. I asked for a ferret. He said no. I asked for a gerbil. He said yes, and we bought a gerbil and took it home. That was my first gerbil and I named him Walnut. Then Dad moved to Cody, Wyoming, and it was hard for Mom to yell at him long distance, but I associate the stoppage of yelling with my gerbil. It was like Walnut was the catalyst for the yelling to be over.

So maybe it's not so unusual that my mind switches to gerbils when things get stressful. I know that other people don't understand this, and so I try not to be too obvious about the relief I get from thinking and talking about gerbils. Still, if everyone had a topic that they could use to their advantage, wouldn't the world be a smarter place with everybody calmly operating with their highest possible IQ?

Harold Pinter is a Pallid Gerbil, a species from North Africa. He is slightly smaller than most other gerbils, with mildly protruding, large dark eyes, and his coat is light orange with a white belly. He has long feet and his tail, barely furred, is longer than his body. His ears are naked. Pallid Gerbils can live two to four years, and so the best-case scenario is that he lives until I am almost twenty-two. I asked for a boy gerbil because that is the pattern of my gerbils: boy, girl, girl, boy, and now, with number five, I am starting again with a boy. Harold Pinter lives in a cage full of wood shavings that I change on a regular basis; I also make sure he has clean sand available, as he bathes in it, much like people bathe in water. I myself hate being in water, and since my biology textbook calls water the solvent of life, I have disliked bathing even more, but my mother has assured me that water won't dissolve any part of me except caked-on dirt and oils. My physical reaction to the bathtub is claustrophobia, as if my skin can't get enough air, and I get a stinging sensation from the shower. I wish that I could take dry baths, like Harold Pinter. It must be nice never to be wet.

The best thing about Harold Pinter is that he likes to be held. I cup him gently in my hand and he trembles with joy. His vibrating is like a cat's purring. I make sure never to sneak up on him, because he startles easily, and can jump straight up, inevitably falling down again due to gravity. Falling could cause him a lot of suffering.

I gave him his name as soon as I got him. I thought it was strange that the idea of naming him after Harold Pinter the playwright didn't bother me, because I usually don't like it if people's names are the same or even similar, but I don't know Harold Pinter the playwright and,

Beverley Brenna

anyways, it would be impossible to get my gerbil mixed up with him. People, on the other hand, could easily become mixed up with each other. As I bike to the university, I try to imagine Harold Pinter asleep in his cage, but even though that thought is comforting, I can still see my mother looking at me, disappointed. And the worst of it is, I am disappointed in myself. The two layers of disappointment stick together, and they aren't happy birthday layers. Even if I try, I cannot seem to separate them, although I know separating them would make the unhappy feeling get smaller. I stop and get off my bike because my eyes have stopped working. I drag the bike over onto someone's lawn and sit down under a tree. The grass beneath my hands feels cool, and when I blindly lay my cheek against it, I think I can feel the world slowly turning. I know this is impossible, but sometimes, when I'm in this extreme state of misery, I hear and see things that are very surprising to someone as logical as I usually am.

"Are you all right?" a voice asks.

"Yes," I say. "I'm resting."

"You're resting?" says the voice.

"Yes," I say.

"You're not hurt?"

"No," I say. "Just trying not to fall off."

"Fall off what?" says the voice.

"The world," I say.

"Yeah, I know what you mean," the voice says. "Life will do that to any of us."

Mom and I watched a movie about Littleman, a character in a sixties British musical, who felt that the world was spinning out of his control. It was called *Stop the World, I Want to Get Off*, and I think that Littleman and I have two things in common. We want control, and we notice its absence.

"I'm glad you're not hurt," says the voice. "I thought you'd had a spill."

"Well, it's not like I'm going to be drinking anything when I'm biking," I say, sitting up and accidentally looking over at the person who is speaking. I almost never look at a person I do not know. It is a guy, and he is looking at me from the driver's side of a car that he is sitting in on the wrong half of the street near where I am.

"You are on the wrong side of the road," I say. "This is not England."

He blinks. He has hazel eyes, a little like Harold Pinter's, and a pale, thin face.

"I just backed this way from the driveway," he says, "to see if you were hurt."

"I'm not hurt," I say. "And you are breaking the law."

"Aren't you in my biology class?" he asks. "You sit in

Beverley Brenna

the corner seat at the front?"

"Maybe," I say. "I am going there now. As soon as I get up, I am going there."

"Well, you're going to be late," he says, "because the class is starting in five minutes. I'm running late because of my brother. He's in the house, but you can probably hear him."

"You don't look like you're running," I say, "and you shouldn't blame your problems on someone else." I stand up and pull my bike out from under the tree and onto the street.

"Wait, I'll give you a ride," he calls, waving his hand. I don't know why he's waving; I don't even know his name.

"I can easily get there in five minutes," I say loudly. "And you'll be lucky if you get there at all. I am thinking that you will never find a place to park." As I bike away, I hear wailing sounds coming from the house. I surmise that the sounds are coming from his brother or a brown capuchin monkey.

Chapter Five

BIOLOGY CLASS

I make it to class with thirty-two seconds to spare, according to my atomic watch, which is always correct. I see the guy I met earlier arrive seventeen minutes into the class. He looks red in the face and takes a seat in the back row. I'm glad I don't have to sit near the back. The seat I like best is in the front row of the lecture theater, left corner, and I like it because if I need to think for a minute and not see anyone else, I can turn my body so that all I see is the wall. It is a gray wall with no pictures on it. This class has 220 students, and sometimes I don't want to look at any of them.

I wonder if he will have to speak to the professor about being late. In high school, our teachers were very strict when it came to lates and absences. My English teacher, Mrs. Thomson, told us that we had to bring a medical certificate or a death notice explaining any absences or lates. It wasn't logical that we would have to bring in our own death notice, though. After all, if we were dead, we would not be going to class. We would not be going anywhere. But I have learned that a lot of things in life are not logical and I did not complain about this policy to Mrs. Thomson.

Today's class is on the composition of cells, or what Dr. Henry calls aqueous cytoplasm. It still makes me feel a little uncomfortable that her gender is female and she has a name like Henry. I know it is her last name, but it just doesn't seem to fit. I find out that cells consist of salts, carbohydrates, lipids, proteins, and nucleic acids. Lipids are a large and diverse group of naturally occurring organic compounds that are related by their solubility in nonpolar organic solvents. Nucleic acids are *macromolecules* composed of chains of *monomeric nucleotides*. In *biochemistry* these molecules carry *genetic information* or form structures within *cells*. I remember learning about the other parts of cells from high school biology.

Most of the information in this class is presented in visual form, which I like because I have an excellent visual memory. This is one of the positive aspects of having Asperger's Syndrome. Something about my brain makes remembering pictures very easy. My favorite part of the class is when Dr. Henry identifies the linear and cyclic structural formulas of glucose. I like the way these formulas look because they make me think of Santa Claus (Ho Ho Ho):

The linear and cyclic structural formulas of glucose.

$$CHO - \underset{\underset{H}{|}}{\overset{\overset{OH}{|}}{C}} - \underset{\underset{OH}{|}}{\overset{\overset{H}{|}}{C}} - \underset{\underset{H}{|}}{\overset{\overset{OH}{|}}{C}} - \underset{\underset{H}{|}}{\overset{\overset{OH}{|}}{C}} - CH_2OH$$

Then I start thinking about Christmas and this makes me a little dizzy because I know Christmas is a long time away and I shouldn't be thinking about it now because today is only Friday, October 4. Soon I'm feeling as if the world is turning under me again and I am on the edge. I grab the corners of my desk, for stability, but my thoughts keep spinning out of control. First we have to have Thanksgiving, and when I think of this, I remember

Beverley Brenna

that I am going to visit my father and I start feeling even more anxious. My last visit there was at Christmastime and I ended up coming home early because I was having a difficult time adjusting. I hope I will not have trouble adjusting at Thanksgiving, but I am not so sure. Cody, Wyoming, where my father lives, is not the same as Saskatoon, Saskatchewan.

I look at the wall for a few minutes. It is still gray. I relax a little. It's a relief when you have a gray wall to face. I stop thinking about Christmas and Thanksgiving and, when I turn back to Dr. Henry, she is talking about steroids. Steroids, she says, are composed of cholesterol and the sex hormones estrogen and testosterone.

I think about Samuel Beckett's play and I wonder if he really meant Estrogen when he named one of his characters Estragon. The class starts talking about a recent newspaper article on an Olympic athlete who is accused of ingesting illegal steroids. If I were an athlete, I would follow the rules. Someone should have made sure this athlete understood the rules because maybe he made a mistake. If he actually took the steroids, that is. You're innocent unless proven guilty.

I turn around and look at the guy in the back row. He is looking up at the clock. You shouldn't look at the clock during class. It's a signal to the professor that you are bored and wish time would speed up so class will be over. Time cannot speed up, though. It is completely predictable, especially if you are wearing an atomic watch that is always correct. Which I am. It is exactly 2:30 PM. Break time. Before we are released for our break, Dr. Henry gives us an outline of what will be on our unit exam next week. I am starting to feel anxious about the unit exam. I am also feeling anxious because after the test is Thanksgiving, and I will be going to Cody, Wyoming. And then, after that, when I come back into this classroom, there will be a different instructor here. This biology class goes all year, and there are four different instructors. I am not sure I will like this class after Dr. Henry is gone, even though she is a lady and her name is supposed to be a man's.

When Dr. Henry tells us to take a ten-minute break, I go to the machine in the hallway, put in a dollar, and get out a 7-Up. The bubbles are sharp in my mouth and it is amazing that anything that feels like this doesn't have corners. Pop always helps me to stay alert and I hope I will be acutely conscious for the rest of the class. As I am drinking, I notice the guy who was late, attempting to get something out of the machine. He is shaking it and swearing.

"You need to put in a dollar," I say, trying to be helpful.

"I did!" he answers. "It just isn't working!"

"Did you press the button?" I say.

"Yes, of course, I pressed the flippin' button," he says, but then he presses a button and out comes a can.

"I bet you didn't press the button," I say. "That's what sometimes happens to me. I always think I did but maybe it was last time."

"Never mind, I've got it now," the guy says. "Except it's a diet one." He sounds cross. I can't tell by looking at his face, but his voice has got a lot of downward inflections in it.

"Are you having a bad day?" I ask.

"I guess you could call it that," he says, opening the pop and taking a long drink. Root beer leaks from his mouth and goes onto the front of his shirt. "*The world is too much with us,*" he mutters, "*late and soon, getting and spending, we lay waste our powers*. Written by William Wordsworth in 1807." Hearing him say this is very unusual. I like to talk about things that happened in the past, but I don't usually bring up things that happened 195 years ago.

"I can tell by the swearing that you are having a bad day," I say. "My dad calls it letting off steam, which is the hydraulic metaphor for releasing emotion."

He does not answer.

"When you let off steam, you feel better," I add.

"Very interesting," says Dr. Henry, who has come up behind us. "There are cognitive neuro-scientific theories about swearing. Have you heard of them?" She puts a dollar into the machine and presses the button to get a Coke.

"No," I say, and my classmate shakes his head, which is another way of saying he hasn't heard about them, either.

"Some scientists have revived Darwin's suggestion that verbalized outbursts are the missing evolutionary link between animals and people. Between, for example, primate shrieking and human language," she says. "Ask me about it later when we have more time."

She takes the can of Coke from the machine.

"So by swearing, you're actually proving your superiority to animals," she says, and goes back into the classroom.

"That's a weird idea," my classmate says.

"I am not sure it is an idea at all," I say. "I think it's just a hypothesis."

He goes back toward the classroom and I follow.

The way he walks, kind of shuffling back and forth, makes me think of someone doing the fox-trot. We have learned this dance in the dance class that I am taking on Sunday afternoons at church. It is not actually church anymore when we are dancing, because the minister is missing.

"Hold on!" I call out to the guy. I have learned that this doesn't refer to holding anything, but actually means, "Stop."

The guy stops and turns around.

"What's your name?" I ask.

"Luke," he says. "Luke Phoenix. What's yours?"

"Taylor Jane Simon," I say, catching up to him. "We'd better go sit down. We don't want to be late. At least I don't want to be late. You don't want to be repeatedly late."

His mouth curves up into what I think is a smile.

"And was that your brother wailing back there," I ask, "or a brown capuchin monkey?"

He laughs.

"My brother," he says. "Martin."

At the end of the class, Dr. Henry asks if anyone has any questions.

"What did you mean when you said that verbalized outbursts were an evolutionary link between people and animals?" I say.

"Oh, you're referring to what we were talking about during the break," she answers. "Well, swearing can be thought of as a response cry. Animals use response cries as part of something called the rage circuit. They use these response cries in situations where they are in pain, to defend themselves and escape from predators. When you drop something on your foot, your body goes into the traditional rage circuit, and you yell out a swear word as your response cry. As a human being, you have shaped your response cry with language. That is why it comes out as a swear word rather than a howl."

"Oh," I say.

"So the human response cry may not actually be a flooding of emotion outwards, as people suggest when they call it 'letting off steam.' It may be a flooding-in of relevance. Of proving to the world that you have more cognition and control than our evolutionary ancestors. Instead of shrieking your pain or irritation at the vending machine"—she nods toward Luke Phoenix—"you used a standard swear word, shaped by your situation. Cathartic, yes, but also very much a part of your evolved intelligence," she adds.

"Thank you," he says, and laughs. "I hadn't thought I was proving my superiority."

"Well, superiority to the primates," she says, and laughs as well.

"I wonder if monkeys ever have bad days," I say.

"Do you mean, 'Are they aware of sequences of negative events?'" says Dr. Henry. "Very good question. I don't think primates mark time in the same way humans do. We are, in the animal kingdom, quite unique." She stops talking and people shut their books. The class is over.

"Okay, I am having a bad day," says Luke Phoenix as we walk down the hall. "I admit it, even if it's just to separate myself from the lower mammals." I think he's going to laugh again, but he doesn't.

"Some days are like that," I say, "Even in Australia." He doesn't answer. Maybe he hasn't read that book, the one where this little kid has a terrible horrible no good very bad day and wants to move to Australia. The message in that book is that you can't escape bad days—they can happen anywhere. I look at Luke Phoenix. I have to try hard to remember that everyone doesn't have the same experiences—that I might have read a book that Luke Phoenix may not have even heard of.

"Even in Australia," I repeat, trying to decide if he's read the book or not.

"I guess so," he says, and presses the button on the vending machine on his way past.

I think he hasn't read the book.

Suddenly, a can falls out of the machine.

"Another diet one!" he says. "But I guess I shouldn't look a gift horse in the mouth." He picks it up and opens it. When he takes a drink, the root beer leaks out of his mouth and drips onto the front of his shirt. I do not know anything about gift horses but when I look it up on the internet, I see that what he really meant was, "Don't be ungrateful when a gift comes along."

Chapter Six

DANCE CLASS

It is Sunday, October 6, and when I go to dance class, I see that, once again, there are not enough men. That is why I keep telling my mother that dancing is a competitive sport, but I do not think she understands.

The women stand along one wall, and the men stand along the opposite wall, and then we have to walk toward each other. Any woman who doesn't get a man has to turn and grab another woman, and then the taller of the two women will take the man's part in the next dance. Today, I move very fast, and so I get a man.

I have learned not to mind being touched by strangers in dance class. When I was in elementary school, before I knew my diagnosis, I used to have meltdowns about being touched, and other kids called me "The Freaker." The worst meltdowns happened in grade five when we were doing square dancing. I did not want my partners touching me but, as this is part of square dancing, they

Beverley Brenna

would touch me anyways. I would allow it for a little while and then I would yell. Eventually, my teacher let me miss square dancing and asked me to clean out the teachers' supply room with the help of a teacher associate named Janet. I enjoyed putting the colored paper back into boxes and organizing things, but I didn't ever learn to square dance.

The next year, when I was in grade six, I had a new teacher associate named Shauna. She and I sometimes talked about my Asperger's Syndrome, because by then my mother had told me why I thought and felt some things differently from most other people. In gym class that year, we did jiving, and Shauna helped me to understand that I could touch a boy's hand while I was dancing with him, and then, later, I could wash my hands if remembering the hand-holding made me worry about germs. I have very smart hygiene about hand-washing. Probably because of this, I am almost never sick. In fact, I have never missed any of my biology classes, which will make writing the unit exam much easier. I am glad, though, that I learned to dance with boys. I am sure that when I have a boyfriend, he will want to hold my hand. Luckily, I will remember the way to do this from dancing.

Today in dance class, I dance with a man whose name is Clifford. I know this because we wear name tags, and that name is on his. I have danced with him before. He is four inches taller than me. He has a big furry mustache that sits on his top lip. At first I stared at it because I thought it was just glued there. Now I think it must be real because no matter what he does, the mustache does not fall off.

"How are you today?" he asks.

How is one of those words that I can't define. It's best not to think about it, and so I just focus on the answer part, which I have been taught.

"Fine," I say.

He nods. It is the answer he expects. People all like things that are predictable—and not just people with autism, either.

When people used to ask me this question, I would focus on the, "Are you," part, and answer with my name. "Yes, I'm Taylor," I'd say.

Then they'd repeat the question: "How are you?"

"I'm Taylor," I'd answer. "I'm Taylor today and Taylor tomorrow, too."

Sometimes they'd laugh or just pause and stare at me. Finally my mother insisted that I just say, "Fine," and be done with it.

First we practice the fox-trot. Slow, slow, quick-quick. I am quite smart at it, but Clifford is not. He keeps stepping on my feet and then he shakes his head and apologizes, but his mustache doesn't move even when he talks.

"Stay off my feet," I warn him, but he doesn't listen and keeps trampling me.

After a while, we change partners. Everyone stops dancing, and then the women stand still while the men, or women pretending they are the men, move to their next partner along the line of dance.

This time I get a girl for a partner. She has very bad breath and I try not to breathe in.

"All right?" she asks, holding up her hands.

"Only if you don't breathe out," I say.

Her name is Tamara and I have not danced with her before. She is taller than I am so she has to pretend to be the man. She also has very weak wrists and does not grip me properly.

"You should take charge," I say. "I do not know where you want me to go unless you direct me to move there."

"I'm tired of being the man," she says. "I was the man last time, too."

"Next time you should run for them," I say. "I have never been the man because I make sure I move fast when we choose our partners."

"You always get Clifford," she says. "I'm married to him, so it isn't fair that I never get him for a partner."

"You can have him for a partner at home," I say. "Here, the fastest one wins. I am fast because I stay in shape and go for long walks."

Soon the dance is over, and we change partners again. This time I get another man. His name is Ohad.

"Hello, how do you do?" he says.

"Do what?" I ask.

"Hello, how do you do?" he says, again.

I am tired of trying to figure him out, so I just say, "Taylor," and he nods, as if I have answered the question correctly. We do not talk for the rest of the dance, and this is just the way I like it.

"It was my pleasure," he says, when we are finished dancing.

"You are smart at not stepping on my feet," I say.

Then we switch partners. My partner is not wearing a name tag and I am not sure if he or she is a man or a woman, but I do not worry about this for long because soon the instructor tells everyone to stop dancing.

"We are going to try the tango," says the instructor. "A few of you requested that we learn some of the basic steps."

We walk away from our partners and the women all line up again, facing the men. We try our steps by ourselves for four minutes, and then we go back to our partner and try the steps with the partner. I cannot

Beverley Brenna

remember where my feet should go. My partner is no help. Plus he or she keeps trying to talk to me.

"What do you do?" he or she asks.

"I am doing the tango," I say, and my voice is beginning to go up the loudness scale.

"No, I mean what do you do when you are not dancing," he or she says.

"I stand still," I say, stepping on one of his or her feet.

"Do you have a job?" he or she asks.

"I don't know," I say, and then I feel miserable.

I might have a job. I might not. But do I have one right now? It is a question that my mother and I care very much about, and every time she looks at me, she has that H of wrinkles in her forehead that means she's worried. The manager of the bookstore hasn't called. This might be positive, because maybe she hasn't called because she's waiting until somebody else types a piece of paper called a contract that I have to sign before I can work there. This might be bad news because maybe she feels sad about calling me to tell me I didn't get the job. And, depending on what I decide, I might say no even if she offers me the job. Thinking of all these things makes me step on my partner's feet again.

"I am studying at the university," he or she says, moving out of reach of my feet.

"Oh," I say. "I am taking a class during the week. It is biology."

"Uh huh," he or she says. "Do you find it interesting?" Now he or she steps on my left foot. It hurts so much I want to swear, but I don't.

"I am interested in the chemical basis for life's kinship," I say, trying to keep my feet away so they will not get stepped on again. "Harold Pinter and I have more in common than one might think."

We keep dancing and I bite the inside of my cheek so that I will not say anything more about my gerbil. The tango is a very hard dance and I will have to figure out the steps before I come back to dance class. After we are told to change partners, I go to the washroom and splash water on my face. In the mirror, my cheeks are very pink. I know that someone will not have a partner right now, and that this will be my fault. I feel like screaming and banging on the sink, but instead, I run some more water on my hands and try to think about breathing. After a while, I am calm again, and I go back onto the dance floor, but the dancing is all over.

"See you after Thanksgiving," says one of the instructors.

"Maybe," I say. "And maybe not."

Beverley Brenna

Chapter Seven

THE TRIP TO WYOMING

A lot has happened since Sunday, October 6, and the dance class. The thing that I don't want to remember is that I had a message to return the phone call of the bookstore manager. I put the note on my dresser and left it there. I still haven't decided what to tell her. Because I haven't decided, I'm going to postpone talking to her. It's difficult talking to someone when you don't know what to say.

The thing that I want to remember is that I wrote the biology unit test and I am sure I will get a smart mark. I knew the answers to all the questions. The only problem was that I knew answers to other questions that weren't on the test, and this bothered me so much that I wrote those answers down on the back of the question sheets that I handed in. I wrote so much that I got a blister on my finger.

Luke Phoenix was handing in his exam at the same

time as I was putting down my question sheets and answer sheets on the professor's table.

"Pity the trees," he said. "*I think that I shall never see a poem as lovely as a tree*. Joyce Kilmer, 1914."

"Kilmer's poem was written eighty-eight years ago," I mutter, thinking that Luke Phoenix is making no sense at all. Firstly, we are indoors, and secondly, even though the class is about biology, we have not spent any time talking about trees. Or poems. I think maybe Luke Phoenix has a mental health problem. Possibly his brother has one, as well, or he wouldn't be wailing all the time. I heard him when I biked past their house all last week, and if Luke hadn't told me differently, I would have expected that the sound was actually coming from a brown capuchin monkey.

The reason I know so much about brown capuchins is because my mother has a tape of them from the honeymoon trip she and Dad took to the San Diego Zoo. All the animals at the zoo are recorded on the tape, and the loudest of them all is the brown capuchin.

I don't know why they have this recording. There used to be pictures to go with it but Mom burned them after Dad left. She took them down into the basement and lit a match, along with some newspaper, until all that was left on the cement floor was a pile of ashes. I thought the house was going to burn down, but it didn't. So all I have

Beverley Brenna

left from their honeymoon is this tape of animal sounds. I found it one day when I was sorting through things in our storage room.

The names on the cover of the tape gave me a surprise. Penelope and Garth Simon. At first I didn't know who *Penelope* was. I'd always thought my mom's name was Penny. I was upset about this for eight days, and I kept playing the tape over and over because there were voices on it, and I wanted to make sure what my mom was telling me was true—that the voice on there really was her. Finally, I determined that it was. But by this time, the animal sounds had become pleasant to listen to, and every now and then I play the tape just to hear them.

It is Friday, October 11, and I am on the bus to Cody, Wyoming. I have a round-trip ticket that my father—Garth Simon—sent to me, and a lunch that my mom pushed into my hand at the last minute. A round-trip is when you go away and then come back. A better name for it would be a boomerang trip. On this half of my boomerang trip to Cody, Wyoming, I won't get to my destination until midnight. That is not a smart time to arrive anywhere, but if I am lucky, I will nap for part of the journey. Most of the people on this bus are gamblers and they have chartered this bus to go to Cody, Wyoming, for the weekend so that they can gamble. I hope that people do not think I am a gambler if they see me on this bus.

I already felt stressed when I woke up this morning because today's schedule is different. My biology class, which I usually have on Fridays, is canceled because the professor has to go to the wedding of her son. When Dr. Henry informed us of this, I felt quite indignant. I think that if you are a professor, and there is a wedding, your class should take priority. Because the class was canceled, I was able to leave home this morning, and get to Cody, Wyoming, at 12:00 AM on Saturday. So this is what I planned to do, as a result of the canceled class, and now I am doing it.

I wonder what my father will look like when I get there. I hope he will look like someone I recognize. I haven't seen him since last Christmas, and he might have changed a lot since then. He might have gotten his hair cut. He might have gained weight. Or lost weight. He might have bought some new clothes. I hope he doesn't wear anything yellow.

On the seat beside me is my Roots travel bag that my mom bought from Avon, and Harold Pinter is in it. I know I am not supposed to bring him on the bus, but I would rather have Harold Pinter with me than any of my clothes. So I brought him instead of my clothes.

Beverley Brenna

His cage fits perfectly inside the bag, with my biology textbook on top. My mom was supposed to feed him while I was gone, but she forgets things like that, so it is smart that I have brought him. This way he won't starve to death. Of course, I did not tell my mother that I was bringing Harold Pinter on the bus. She would have strongly objected because she has never let me bring any of my other gerbils on trips. She says that gerbils are not meant for traveling, and that is why I am bringing him secretly. I think she is wrong about Harold Pinter. He is taking this trip very calmly. I unzip the bag just enough so fresh air gets in, and I can see him snuggled down in a little nest of wood shavings on one side of the cage. Although I want to put my hand inside the cage and pet him, I refrain. There are some things you are definitely not supposed to do on buses, especially if you have a gerbil that is a secret.

It took me a long time to understand about secrets. When I was a kid, I didn't understand the possibility of thinking something that nobody else knew. That's part of knowing about perspective-taking. The idea that someone could have a different perspective than me used to be confusing.

When I stop to calculate, I realize that I have spent over fifty percent of my life confused and afraid. I am trying not to let my emotions boss me around, though. Last summer, I saw a play that made me think about being bossed around. Stanley, in the play, was afraid of so many things that he just stayed in his room at the boarding house. I'm afraid of a lot of things, too, but I try not to be like Stanley. He was so afraid that he stopped doing things. He stayed dormant inside his room and let his landlady control his life. All she would give him to eat was cereal and he didn't like cereal. I have resolved not to be like this. I am not going to let my emotions or even my mom boss me around. I would not like to eat cereal every day, especially Corn Flakes. I eat fourteen mouthfuls of my mom's lunch. She has packed my favorite foods. She has also packed an apple, because she likes apples, but I am not going to eat it. There are a couple of pancakes and I eat them first. Then I drink some water from my water bottle with the straw, and this makes me feel calm, even though I am on a bus with a lot of gamblers, heading in a direction I can't exactly identify, although my brain tells me we're going south. After that, I eat two hard-boiled eggs, and then I worry a bit about Harold Pinter. Does he have enough food and water? I put my head down and peek into his cage, through the place where the zipper is open. He still has pellets, and I see water in his water bottle, which should make me feel relieved, except I still

Beverley Brenna

feel anxious. I feel that my anxiousness could get very big and I quickly sit up in my seat and look out the window, trying to take deep breaths. Sometimes this helps and sometimes it doesn't. Luckily, this time it helps.

It is very smart of me to be thinking about Harold Pinter at a time like this, because traveling on the bus is very unsettling. There is a hungry sensation in my stomach that I know is not hunger. It is the feeling I get when I am ready to throw up, but I know that I will not throw up right now. Right now, I am opening and closing the zipper of my bag and studying my gerbil. As long as I think about Harold Pinter, I know I can manage. When I walked along the platform at the bus station and said goodbye to my mother, I was really counting my steps so that I would know the distance to get on the bus, and, at the same time, I was thinking about my gerbil and wondering if maybe he was taking many little steps inside his cage while I was taking big steps outside the bus. It took me thirty-three steps to walk down the platform, and four steps to climb the stairs into the bus, and then twelve more steps down the aisle to find my seat, and all this made forty-nine, which is a very lucky number because seven squared is forty-nine.

When we reach the border between Canada and the United States, we have to get off the bus so that an inspector can come on and do an inspection. After twenty-six minutes in the bus station, we are allowed to get back on the bus. I feel anxious when I sit down, and I keep my head lowered as I check to make sure Harold Pinter is okay. By the time the bus starts moving, I am feeling more relaxed and I sit up straight. When I look around, I notice that every seat on the bus has someone sitting in it except for the seat beside me and two seats at the front. One person is staring at me. I can't tell if it's a woman or a man, but the person is wearing a brown leather coat and wire spectacles. I smile to myself. I used to be afraid of seeing people wearing glasses. No one in my family wears glasses, and so I wasn't exposed to them very early. Once, when a teacher at school got glasses, it freaked me out. I thought something was wrong with her eyes, and seeing her like that, so different, made me feel as if everything else at school was going to be different, and I remember yelling and kicking things. That was before people knew I had Asperger's Syndrome and so I just got sent home.

When I look across the aisle, the person is still staring at me. Didn't this person's mother ever say it isn't polite to stare? I turn back to the window and look out into the night. Darkness is an easy thing to watch. It doesn't fall, just as Estragon says in the play, and it is a lie when people say "nightfall." Darkness arrives gradually. You can look at it as long as you want and it doesn't remind you of anything. The only problem is, darkness isn't permanent. Dawn comes, and the minister at church says it is always darkest just before dawn.

After my eyes feel rested, I look at my watch. It is 8:39. I think I must have slept for one hour. Then the numbers change. Now it is 8:40. Numbers are one thing I can count on. Or rather, numbers are one thing I can count with.

I start wondering if there are any other ways to count things, in case numbers aren't available. This thought makes me feel a little sick to my stomach. There really isn't a backup plan for numbers, and now I'm feeling anxious again. The feeling is really big, now, and I stand up and go to the washroom at the end of the bus. Once I've squeezed in there, I splash water on my face and then dry myself with a paper towel. The door has shut behind me, and I can't figure out a way to make it open. I start to panic. If I don't get out of this tight space, I'm going to use up all the air and die. I flail my arms and legs and suddenly think of Dr. Henry talking about the rage circuit. Is that what's happening to me? This is the last conscious thought I have until I find myself lying across a set of leather seats that smell like hard-boiled eggs and human sweat.

I sit up. There is a person standing in the aisle, leaning over me. It is an older person with white hair.

"Are you okay, now?" the person says. It is a woman because she has the figure of a woman.

"Yes," I say. "I think so."

"Were you stuck in there for very long?" she asks. I look at my watch. It is 8:51.

"Possibly three minutes," I say. "Just long enough to stop breathing if you don't have enough air."

She lightly pats me on the shoulder and I pull away.

"Well, I can never figure those things out," she says. "They want you to push the knob a certain way, but who's to know? The doors are all different, and even if you figure out one of the jiggers, there'll be another one that doesn't work the way you expect."

I'm not sure exactly what she means, but she is smart to notice that doors are all different. I have noticed that, as well. It would make more sense to have everything the same, and then you would not have to spend time learning something you are only going to use once.

I realize that the seat I am lying across is my own. I squeeze my hand into the Roots bag until it rests on top of Harold Pinter's cage. It will be comforting for him to see my hand. The person across the aisle in the leather jacket gets up, takes down a suitcase from the overhead rack, and goes to the front of the bus. I wonder what is in that suitcase. I hope that it is not a gerbil, because there aren't any openings for air.

I have made it. I am in my room at Dad's. It was seventy-seven steps from the bus to his car. The last step was a big one, but I wanted to finish in sevens. This is the first time I have taken a bus journey by myself. It occurs to me to pat myself on the back, although I know that this is just something people say rather than do. I am doing it, though. It feels pleasant.

My watch is on the shelf beside the bed. Harold Pinter's cage is sitting on the floor in the corner and he is in it, curled up inside his toilet paper tube. It is nighttime and he is supposed to be getting rambunctious, but I think the bus journey disturbed his daytime sleep. He is sleeping now. He has his paws scrunched up over his eyes as if he does not want to see the world. My biology textbook is on top of the cage, for maximum safety.

"It's okay," I tell him. "Sleep as long as you want to. It's a holiday. Sort of." I hope Harold Pinter does not have a sleep disorder.

What bothers me most is that it isn't Thanksgiving here in Cody, Wyoming. In Canada, Thanksgiving is the second Monday in October, but in the United States, it is the fourth Thursday in November. So while I am in Cody, Wyoming, I am actually missing Thanksgiving. Dad said we could have turkey on Sunday night if I wanted, but I don't. I dislike turkey. I just like a consistency in holidays.

I climb into bed and pull up the covers, but it is hard to sleep in a different place. I can hear sounds I don't hear at home. Like Dad snoring. I never hear that at home because Dad isn't there. He's here in Cody, Wyoming and he keeps his snoring with him.

I can't remember if he used to snore. That could be one of the ways he's different from before. His face is still the same, though: his mouth, where there are little wrinkles around the edges when he smiles, looks familiar. He's definitely still the same person, even though he snores. Although now he looks like Cat Stevens. I remember seeing Cat Stevens's picture on the front of a CD. Cat Stevens has curly, longish dark hair with streaks of gray, and dark eyes. When I saw Dad at the bus station, instead of thinking, "That's my dad, Garth Simon," I thought, "That's Cat Stevens." It's strange that one person can look like another person.

As I lie here in the dark, I feel as if I am waiting for something. *What am I waiting for?* Maybe I am waiting for Godot, like the other characters in Samuel Beckett's play, because I have a sense that they do not know what

Beverley Brenna

they are waiting for either, and therefore their experience is parallel to mine. But at least they are waiting together, while I have no one. I am waiting alone.

I wish that in life I could just move along the line of dance and find a partner. In Waskesiu, last summer, I had one boyfriend, and maybe two, but only for a very short time. In my estimate, one was my boyfriend for one day, and the other for just a few seconds. My mother has had lots of boyfriends, and I think that getting boyfriends is one of her strengths. Unfortunately, I did not inherit this skill, just as I did not inherit her brown eyes and blonde hair. And, just as unfortunately, life is not dance class.

I wonder if Luke Phoenix is celebrating Thanksgiving with his family and I wonder if his brother is still wailing like a monkey. Then I wonder if Luke Phoenix is lying in bed, alone, just like I am, and if this makes me less alone. But you can't be more or less alone, it's all or nothing. I look around in the dark room. I am definitely all alone.

Waiting for No One

Chapter Eight

THANKSGIVING WEEKEND

Today is Saturday, October 12, and we are at a rodeo. It is not the first rodeo I have been to, and I do not think it will be the last. Six years ago, when Mom and I came to visit Dad in Cody, Wyoming, I was twelve and that was my first rodeo. That rodeo was on a Saturday, too. Saturday, October 12, 1996. I did not expect to enjoy the rodeo then, but I did.

Today we have to buy tickets at a store on Main Street. Then we walk around town, looking in the windows of places where people are gambling at arcades. I am very surprised to see that all the shops have arcades. People must win money or they wouldn't play so much. Unless they are addicted. I know you can get addicted to gambling in the same way you can get addicted to smoking. Both gambling and smoking are bad. I ask my father if he ever gambles or smokes, and he says, "That's just not my bag."

"I don't see any bags," I say.

"That's just an expression, Taylor," my dad answers. "It means it's not my cup of tea. Like, it means ... uh ... it's not something I care to do." Then he says that he doesn't have money to burn. It's not actually the money that you're burning when you light a cigarette, but I don't tell him this. And anyways, what does burning have to do with gambling?

I remember a DVD we saw in high school about gambling. It showed a man who was addicted and who stole things to support his addiction. He would go into stores and, when he thought nobody would see, he would stuff things into a big black knapsack. Then he would take the things to sell at a pawnshop. If I get the job in the bookstore, I won't let people come in with black knapsacks.

I do not remember these arcades from the last time I was in Cody, Wyoming. I ask my dad if they were just built, and he says no, they were here when he moved here. That was in December, 1992, almost ten years ago.

"When you were younger, I guess we didn't come downtown," Dad tells me.

"I am glad," I say. "I would not have wanted to be influenced by all this gambling. It is bad for you, and kids should not have to see things they could get addicted to."

As we walk past the shops with the arcades, I take little looks in at them but I do not see anyone else from the chartered bus. The arcade games are like giant yellow and gold cash registers with all sorts of buttons and knobs. I see a skinny man with a green T-shirt stand up and yell when the yellow and gold machine he was playing at starts making noises. Then I see money come out of the bottom, in change, and he puts it into his hat. I see a fat person in a yellow T-shirt, sitting at one of the yellow and gold arcades and drinking from a brown bottle. I feel like sneezing, and then I do. I sneeze five times, and then Dad says maybe we should walk in another direction.

At 3:45, we drive to the rodeo grounds and park the car. Then we come inside the stadium, climb up the bleachers past a lot of other people, and sit near the top. I want to sit at the very top, because that is where I sat the last time we were here exactly six years ago, but other people are already sitting there. I could tell them to leave but this is not a smart thing to do. The rodeo starts when riders on horseback charge out with American flags. They ride around the ring and then everyone claps and there is music from a sound system. I can see men down below, getting ready to ride. They take turns getting on the back of a bull that is contained in a tiny pen. After each one gets seated, the bull is let out into the ring. The rider

Beverley Brenna

has to hang onto his hat with one hand and the back of the bull with the other hand. The winner is the man that stays on the longest. It looks hard, and it probably is hard, because the bulls are bucking and going crazy. I think the men have spurs on their heels that dig into the animals' sides. It isn't right for people to go around beating up animals.

One bull in particular is so crazy, I think they might never get him out of the ring. After the rider falls off, the bull bucks itself around in a complete circle, coming right to our side of the ring, and I get a glimpse of the look in his eye. Then I realize he isn't crazy, after all. He's in that state where you're not getting enough oxygen and so parts of your brain shut down. All that's left is fight or flight, and he is trying to do both. The rage circuit.

"He's pretty crazy," my dad says.

"He's trying to save himself," I say. "He just doesn't have the right words."

In four minutes, the bull is calmer because a little terrier has rounded him up, and now he is heading toward one of the pens they have along the side of the ring. When the bull gets into the pen and the gate is shut, he completely settles down. I can tell he feels safe in there. He knows there isn't going to be any more riding inside that pen, and he is glad. I know the way that feels.

When I was in grade two, my teacher had a big cardboard box at the back of the classroom where kids could go and work if they felt like it. I spent a lot of time sitting in one corner of that box to escape the classroom setting. I used to go into the box and count the other corners, and it was very reassuring because there were always seven, in addition to the one I was sitting in. But I'm not going to think about that. The number seven isn't any better than any other number, although sometimes I forget and think it is. It was in grade two when kids started called me "The Freaker." They did not understand why unpredictable things made me freak out. I have thought a lot about this since then, and I am still not happy when I remember those days. Being called by something other than your own name is very unpleasant. Even last summer, when my friend Paul thought I was like a wild orchid, it was still another person trying to label me. Why do people do that? I just want to be myself: Taylor Jane Simon. And when I write about myself, nothing here is made up. Otherwise I would be someone else and that person would be fiction.

At the rodeo, there is an announcer who tells us all about what is happening and gives us facts about the riders. He tells us about men who have come from as far away as Australia. Why would someone come from

Australia to ride a breathless bull around a ring in Cody, Wyoming? I suppose there are bad days, even in Australia, and a person just might want a change of scenery. Even though the announcer tells us all about the riders, he does not tell us anything about the bulls. There is no guarantee of equality at rodeos.

Eventually, there is a contest where the kids all go down from the stands and chase a black calf with a red ribbon on its tail. The first person to get the ribbon wins one hundred dollars. Dad wants me to go down there, but I refuse. I am not a kid anymore and it is embarrassing that he suggests it. Once I get a job, I can earn a hundred dollars easily, so I won't have to rely on contests as a source of income. If I get a job. This thought makes me start feeling afraid and the sum of embarrassment and fear is anger. I reach into my pocket and get out some gum. It's peppermint.

When they let the calf out of his pen, I can see his tail switching back and forth. As soon as he realizes he is out in the open, he starts to buck and struggle and then run. His fear has turned into fury. It isn't right that kids are allowed to chase him when he is mad. When I am mad, the last thing I would want is to be chased. Right now, I am chewing gum and trying to keep my IQ in the triple digits. I hope that this rodeo will be my last. Animals are not meant to be treated like this.

I am still mad after the rodeo is over and we go out for dinner. We drive to a steak house where they do not have pancakes or blueberries on the menu. I order a baked potato and sour cream, but because I am angry, I do not enjoy it. Dad has a steak, a baked potato, a little bowl of baked beans, and a piece of apple pie. He winks at me as he starts eating the pie.

"You are still the apple of my eye," he says, and then he looks down at his plate.

"I am just myself," I say, so there will be no mistake.

I have been wondering if Dad is lonely here all by himself, because people are supposed to need their family to live with, but after dinner, we drive up to a house that isn't his and he stops the car.

"Come on inside, Taylor," he says. "I want you to meet somebody."

"Who?" I say.

"A good friend of mine. A really good friend. She's— well, she's someone that I met at work and we just sort of hit it off."

"Hit what?" I ask.

"We get along good together," he says.

"Oh," I say. "Is she your girlfriend?"

"Yes," he says. "Like that."

Beverley Brenna

"But you don't hit her," I say, "because that would be against the law."

Dad sort of snorts. "I don't hit anyone," he says. "Hitting it off means we get along."

"I don't have to meet her today," I say. "It's kind of late."

"No, she's a night owl; she won't mind," says Dad. For a minute I think he means she really is an owl, and it makes me laugh. I mean, having a gerbil as a friend is one thing, but having an owl as a girlfriend would be something else.

We get out of the car and go up to the door. When he rings the bell, I can hear it play a little tune. Then the door opens and this person is there. She is taller than me and taller than Dad, but not wider.

"What is that song?" I ask.

"'The Star Spangled Banner,' honey, our national anthem," says Dad's girlfriend. Then she says to Dad, "This is one sweet-looking girl"

"This is Sadie Richards," Dad says to me. Then he turns to her. "Sadie, meet my daughter."

"I am Taylor Jane Simon, just myself," I say.

I put out my hand but she leans forward and hugs me with both arms. I step backwards so fast I lose my balance and end up splayed out in the flower bed by the front step.

"Oh, my goodness!" says Sadie Richards. "Ass over teakettle!" And then she laughs, but she stops laughing when I tell her that it isn't appropriate to swear.

When I try to get up, I can't, and I say "Shit" a few times until Dad carefully hauls me to my feet. I feel weak in the knees, which is strange, because it isn't my knees that are hurt. It is my arm.

Dad drives me to the clinic and we cannot go and get Harold Pinter first and they say my arm is not broken but that I probably have a mild strain, which is a pseudonym for a tear of the muscle fiber. I am not sure what the clinic looks like because I keep my eyes mostly shut. I only open them at the end when someone asks if I want a sticker. "Why would I want a sticker?" I say, but no one answers. I believe those stickers are only for children, and if they give me one, it would be breaking the rules. When we get back to Dad's apartment, I spend sixty minutes holding Harold Pinter. He is very capable at calming me down.

Being at the clinic took a long time, so we have to postpone the visit with Sadie Richards until today. So now it is Sunday, October 14, at 10:04 AM, and I am sitting at Sadie Richards's dining room table having breakfast, which is against the rules because you're supposed to eat breakfast in the kitchen. Harold Pinter is in his cage in the living room because I do not want to leave him alone in Dad's apartment on Thanksgiving, even though it is only Sunday and Thanksgiving is officially tomorrow. At least, it is in Canada. This year in the United States, Thanksgiving is on Thursday, November 28. This is not going to be a problem because Dad told me that, since I am going home tomorrow, I will actually be in Canada for Thanksgiving, so I won't miss it. When he said this, I was very relieved.

For breakfast we are eating pancakes. When Sadie Richards asked me what I like to eat, Dad interrupted and said I would eat whatever she was having, but I told her pancakes and she made them. They are not like the ones I'm used to eating but they are okay. I like Sadie Richards, even though she is a hugging type of person and I am not. She has a nice smell. She is also very tall.

"I'm sorry I laughed when you fell off the step," said Sadie Richards.

There is a silence and I think I should say something.

"In dance class, you would get to be the man," I say.

Dad sort of snorts and says, "What kind of a thing is that to tell her?" and I don't really know what he means because it is only words, not anything else.

"And I'm sorry if it was my fault that you fell, honey," says Sadie Richards.

"That's okay," I say. "It is just a mild strain and it doesn't hurt now." I look at my arm. There is a big bruise on the back of the elbow.

Sadie Richards is still looking at me and I feel as if I should say something more.

"I sometimes yell when it is not appropriate," I say. "And swear. Although this time, I think my swearing was understandable. It belonged in the moment of falling off the step in a way that it did not belong during my job interview."

"You've had a job interview?" my dad asks. "No kidding! Where?"

"At the Eighth Street Bookstore," I say. "But I really don't want to talk about it."

Chapter Nine

MORE ABOUT SADIE RICHARDS

Sadie Richards's house is full of interesting things. In the kitchen she has dishes of all different patterns. I can tell she likes each dish for its originality and doesn't want things that come in a set. She told me she bought most of her dishes at garage sales.

"Did you get this plate at a garage sale?" I ask, pointing at the blue china plate under my pancakes.

"That is a very special plate," she says. "I got it from a healing center. The shaman said it had special powers to draw peace and harmony into the home."

"Really?" I say, taking another bite of my pancake. "What does that mean?"

"Well, the color blue is supposed to be cooling and calming. I think it's supposed to detoxify the environment."

"Oh," I say. "I already know that blue is superior. What exactly is a shaman?"

"Someone who is supposed to cure the sick and control events through magic," she says. "Kind of a faith healer."

I eat two more bites of my pancake.

"Taylor, how do you feel about your dad and me?" Sadie Richards asks. "Are you okay with our relationship?"

"I understand that nobody wants to be waiting alone," I say slowly, forking another piece of pancake into my mouth and carefully wiping the syrup from my chin with the back of my wrist.

Dad makes a funny sound in his throat and I look at him to see if he is choking, but he is not. His plate is yellow with a brown ring around the edge.

"Where did you get that plate?" I ask Sadie Richards, trying to look at only the brown parts instead of the yellow.

"I won it at a charity auction," she says. "The auction was to raise money for building wells in Africa. I bought a lot of tickets and when I won that plate, I was happy because when I see it, I think of all those children drinking clean water."

"It has too much yellow in it," I say, and then I sneeze.

Sadie Richards offers me another pancake and I accept it.

"Do you have any golf clubs?" I ask her.

"No," she says.

I wish my mother would pick a boyfriend who buys blue plates from shamans and doesn't like things that come in a set. My mother's boyfriends always have matching golf clubs. I bet if Sadie Richards bought golf clubs, she would buy them at garage sales and they would not have identical handles. My mother picks boyfriends that like identical handles. I have seen them carrying their clubs with identical handles, in black vinyl golf bags. Her boyfriends also like polyester golf shirts that match their pants. I have not liked any of my mother's boyfriends and I am wary of the next one, especially if he is wearing a golf shirt.

Sadie Richards tilts her head a little to one side when I talk. I can tell she is listening to me.

"I'm glad you're okay with your dad and me," she says, eating a piece of pancake off her own plate, which is green.

"I want to hear more about the shaman," I say.

"Well, she lit a pipe. She had some sage grass burning in it. She said my whole name and then she had a kind of vision where she saw a tree and I was under it, and the tree was full of birds."

"You were waiting under the tree?" I ask, thinking about Samuel Beckett's play and the way Vladimir and Estragon waited under a tree for more than just an hour.

"I think so, and there were all these birds above me.

The shaman said that if I listened, I could hear each bird's song."

"Really?" I say. "And could you?"

"I don't know," Sadie Richards says. "It was the shaman's vision, not mine."

"Do you think a shaman really can control events through magic?" I say, thinking about my job interview.

"Not really," says Sadie Richards. "I think that given enough support, though, people can control their own destinies."

"Oh," I say, and then my dad says, "Pass the syrup, please," and I do because I am finished with it. In fact, I am finished with my pancakes and I go into the kitchen and put the plate on the shelf.

"Taylor," Sadie Richards says, "shall we see if that gerbil would like to stretch his legs? He must get tired of being cooped up in that cage. I bet he'd like to be free on the carpet while we have our coffee."

I don't think Harold Pinter likes carpets, and I tell her that we don't let him out because he could get lost, but I let her bring his cage into the dining room and set it down where we can see him. He is sleeping, as usual. Soon he might wake up, but right now he looks as if he is in a very deep sleep. Sadie Richards makes her voice soft so she doesn't wake him.

"Sweet little thing," she croons. "What do you call him again?"

"Harold Pinter," I say, lifting my textbook from the top of the cage. "He has a lot of freedom right now. He has freedom from hunger and thirst, and freedom from fear. He also has freedom to express normal behavior, like chewing things up and making nests. He digs so that he can feel safe in a cozy spot, not because he needs to dig. A gerbil that just keeps digging and digging isn't just obsessed with digging. It's trying to make a cozy spot but probably doesn't have enough material."

I flip open my textbook and start reading a chapter we have not covered yet in class. It is about primates. I read some things about primate diversity and then I read that humans share ninety-nine percent of our genome with chimpanzees, our closest living relatives. Then I read about language; the book says language is a uniquely human trait.

Even though they don't have language, I have read somewhere that chimpanzees can do a lot of impressive things. For example, they can tell the difference between two hundred different kinds of jungle plants, where they grow, and what time of year you can find them there. Unless you observe chimpanzees in their natural setting, you are not going to see this smartness. Just like if you don't give a gerbil enough materials, it will keep digging and digging and look stupid.

"Harold Pinter is the luckiest little gerbil," says Sadie Richards. "I have never had a gerbil, but I once had a potbellied pig and he was very nice. I called him Snout because his nose was at least four inches long, a third the size of his body." I like it that she describes the size of her pig. It is quite exact and this is very satisfying.

"You have picked a smart person for your girlfriend," I tell Dad.

"Thank you," he says, and I think he is smiling, but I'm not looking at him. I would rather look at Harold Pinter, even though he is asleep, because animals are easier to look at than people.

"It is important to have somebody to wait with," I say.

"Why are you talking all the time about waiting?" Dad says.

"People are always waiting," I tell him. "I am waiting to turn nineteen, but after that I will be waiting to turn twenty. I am also waiting to get a job. The manager of the bookstore is waiting for me to call her back. Mom is waiting for me to come home. I'm not sure what you are waiting for, but everyone's waiting for something. And you shouldn't wait by yourself if you have a choice."

"I've missed you, Taylor," Dad says, and there are a lot of little wrinkles around his mouth that I don't think

Beverley Brenna

are from smiling. I know he really did miss me, even if he moved away from home when I was eight and never came back and now looks a lot like Cat Stevens.

"Thank you," I say. "Did you know that parental care is one of the things that separates us from primates? Also bipedalism, a larger brain, and the use of language to represent symbolic thought."

"Bipedalism?" asks Dad.

"Walking upright," I say. "At first I thought it meant riding a bicycle, but it doesn't."

"Would you like to take a drive to Yellowstone Park?" asks my dad.

"No," I say, for obvious reasons.

After coffee, we go out for a walk. We walk all around downtown again, but this time I do not look in the windows at the yellow and gold arcades and the people smoking and gambling. That will just upset me and I want to try and stay calm so that Sadie Richards will like me. I don't look at the mountains, either, as I am not used to seeing mountains and I don't enjoy seeing these, even though one is called Heart Mountain and somewhat resembles the top of a heart.

"Honey," she says as we walk down a street where there are big maple trees with russet-colored leaves, "when we get back, do you want me to put that dress into the washer? It looks like it could use a break."

"Oh," I say, looking down at my dress. "I don't want it broken. It's my favorite."

"No, I mean it looks as if it could use a cleaning," she says. I notice a few spots on the front where I spilled orange juice. And pancake syrup.

"Well, I don't have anything else to change into," I say.

"You can borrow something of mine," she says. "We must be nearly the same size."

I look at her. I know that she is taller than I am. Her mouth looks a lot bigger than mine, too. She reminds me of Julia Roberts in a commercial I have seen about a movie.

"Thank you," I say. I am still trying very hard to be polite.

When we get back it is 3:30 PM. I am hungry because I didn't want a hamburger when Dad and Sadie Richards each had one. I hope there are some pancakes left. Sadie Richards opens the door and we go into the house. I go into the dining room to see Harold Pinter. But I don't see him. He is missing from his cage. My textbook is on the floor where I left it, still open to the page about primates and not on top of the cage where it is supposed to be.

I start to yell and for a little while I don't know what I am doing. I know that I am running into the kitchen and there are a lot of big sounds. Then I realize that my

Beverley Brenna

dad has me around the shoulders in a bear hug and he is pulling me towards the couch. We fall on it together, and luckily I am on the top, but he still has his arms around me and I can't get free.

"Taylor," he is saying. "Take a deep breath. Then another. Calm down."

I look at the top of my hand. It is bleeding. I don't know why. I make some sounds in my throat, and then I think about that bull in its little pen and I take a deep breath and relax my arms and legs.

Sadie Richards comes in with a Kleenex and a Band-aid. Dad lets go of me and while she takes care of the scratch on my hand, I look over her shoulder into the kitchen. There are pieces of broken dishes on the floor.

"Those dishes are broken!" I say, and I can hear that my voice is in the red zone but I can't make it any smaller. "Those dishes are broken!" I yell again. But even though I'm really asking what caused them to break, something inside me knows.

"Hush now, Taylor, you did that when you were letting off steam," my father says. "Time to clean up, and then we'll figure out how you're going to pay Sadie back."

"Do you mean if I'm going to pay her back?" I ask. "Or is it intended that I am going to."

"It's intended," Dad says.

"I'm sorry," I say to Sadie Richards. "I wish I hadn't broken your dishes. That was a very unsmart thing to do. When I'm upset my IQ goes down, and this time I think it went all the way. I have never lost Harold Pinter before." I start to feel myself getting worked up again. "Where is he? Do you know where he could be?"

"Let's look around," says Sadie Richards. "But we'll have to be quiet. If we're noisy, we'll scare him so much he'll never come out. And be careful of your strained arm."

"It isn't sore anymore," I say. "It was yesterday, but it's not now."

I look into the corners of the dining room and then I look around the living room. I check under the couch. I check under the chairs and the china cabinet. I even try to look under the piano, but there's not a lot of room under there.

Dad checks the living room, too, and Sadie Richards looks in the kitchen. All of a sudden, Sadie Richards calls out, "He's here! He's here under the fridge!"

I almost start to yell again. The thought of a small gerbil under a big heavy fridge is frightening. What if he is stuck under there and can't breathe?

Sadie Richards tells me to come and sit in front of the fridge. Then she takes a wooden meter-stick—except she calls it a yardstick—and gently scrapes along at the back of the fridge. All of a sudden, Harold Pinter runs towards me. Hanging out of his mouth is a wilted piece of carrot top. I reach out and cup him in my hands. His body is trembling, and it's not from purring. He's having a meltdown, I can just tell.

I carefully stand up and go back to his cage. Gently, I deposit him into the bed of wood shavings. He scurries into the toilet paper tube and scuffles around for three minutes. Then he eats the rest of the carrot top. He has stopped trembling and he starts washing his face. That is a healthy sign. If he feels like eating and cleaning himself, he can't be that scared. Maybe the carrot tranquilized him. Some plants can do that to animals. It is called zoopharmocobrophy when animals use plants to self-medicate.

"Thank you for finding him!" I say to Sadie Richards.

"He wanted to be found," she says. "He was making these little noises under there. I think he was calling you."

"Maybe he was," I say. "Or maybe he just had to go to the bathroom." Then I laugh, because who ever heard of a gerbil using a bathroom. The next thing is cleaning up. We have to pick up the little pieces of broken dishes and put them into the garbage. At first, as we are gathering the shards of china, Sadie Richards starts telling me about one of the plates that is broken. It had little gold circles on it. She found it a long time

Waiting for No One

87

ago under a pile of records at a garage sale. She says she bought some of the records to play, as well as buying the plate. I do not know what she is talking about until Sadie Richards tells me that records are like big CDs.

"Did they contain baroque music?" I ask. "Like the Brandenburg concertos?"

"Not the records I bought," she says. "I got only folk music in those days. One record I remember was by a singer named Dory Previn. I think it was called *Mythical Kings and Iguanas*. She was way before your time. A really strong environmentalist."

"I remember Dory Previn!" my dad says. "Her songs helped me kind of discover myself when I was in my early twenties."

"How can you discover yourself?" I ask. "You're there all along."

"Maybe," says my father. "And maybe not. They call it *finding yourself* when you're learning about what's important in life. People are pretty complex and, when you're young, you may not really know what makes you tick."

"Oh," I say, looking down at my atomic watch. It does not tick, and it is now 4:25 PM.

"And as soon as I saw the plate with the gold circles at that garage sale," Sadie Richards goes on, "I thought that the circles reminded me of notes, and I wondered if that plate had just absorbed some of the music from the records."

"For real?" I ask.

"No. But it made me think of music, every time I used that plate."

"That's the thing about music," I say. "You can hear it even if you're not really hearing it. You can hear it in your mind, which is very helpful if you're not near anything that can play it to you. Or if the plate that you used to hear it on has broken."

"You should say you're sorry," my father says. "For breaking Sadie's plates."

"I'm sorry," I say in a very quiet voice.

"That makes me think of solo music," Dad says. "So low you can't hear it."

"If that was a joke, I don't get it," I say, but Sadie Richards is already talking about the blue plate.

"Maybe we can glue this one back together," she says. "It's only split into two pieces."

"I hope gluing it will bring harmony back into the home," I say.

"I think it will," says Sadie Richards, and fetches some glue from a cupboard.

"I hope it will," I say.

"My little pig used to eat off the plate with the brown stripe," she tells us. "He especially loved potato peelings."

"What?" says my dad. "The plate I was eating from?"

"Well, it's been washed since," Sadie Richards says, and laughs.

"What was his name again? Snout?" I ask.

"Yes," says Sadie Richards. "I eventually gave him to a petting zoo because I couldn't take care of him when I went away for summer holidays. At least once a year I'd go back to see him, and one year there was this great big, enormous pig in a cage. When I asked about him, I discovered he was Snout's grandson."

"What happened to Snout?" I ask.

"I don't know, but his grandson still lives at that zoo, I think," Sadie Richards says.

"Once my gerbil that was called June got under the kitchen sink," I say. "We used peanut butter to lure her out, but I didn't think of that today."

Then Sadie Richards says she will just vacuum up the rest of any china that is left on the floor.

"And what about the green plate, that you were eating from?" I ask, checking to make sure I did not cut my fingers on the last piece of china that I have found and put into the garbage can. "Where did you get that plate?"

"It belonged to my first husband," says Sadie Richards. "He bought it because he said it made him feel calm. I think that's true, by the way. He did seem calmer when he was near that plate."

"Are there any pancakes left?" I ask.

"No, but I think I have some frozen waffles," says Sadie Richards.

"I'm sorry your husband's green plate is broken," I say as I put two frozen waffles into Sadie Richards's toaster. "Now he won't be able to get calm."

"He's dead," says Sadie Richards. "So he's actually as calm as he can get."

"Oh," I say, and Dad makes this little choking noise in his throat. I pick up a dishrag and start cleaning the shelf. I feel calm again and the cleaning makes me feel even better. After I eat the waffles, I clean every surface in the kitchen, twice, while Sadie Richards vacuums and then talks quietly to Dad in the living room.

"We'd better get going," Dad says, just as I'm starting a third round of cleaning. "Tomorrow we have to get up early to get you to the bus station."

"Okay," I say.

"Do you want a change of clothes?" Sadie Richards asks. "So you can wash your things at your dad's?"

"Yes, please," I say. So that is the way it happened that I am sitting in my dad's apartment, wearing a pink jogging suit and waiting for my jean dress to get dry. I am not feeling very comfortable because I am in Sadie

Richards's clothes and pink is not, as Dad would say, "my bag." This means that I do not care to wear pink. Also, the tag on the back of the top is digging into the nape of my neck. But I know that the dryer will be done in seventeen more minutes and then I can change into my own things. While I am waiting, I use a blue facecloth to wipe the dresser in my room. The dresser doesn't look dirty, but it probably is.

Chapter Ten

HOME AGAIN

It is late Monday night and my mother says that tomorrow morning I have to phone the manager of the Eighth Street Bookstore and return her call. The problem is that I really don't want to talk to her, whatever her name is, but Mom is insisting.

Why doesn't Mom call her if she wants someone to call her? In fact, why doesn't Mom try and work there—see if she likes it? I would not like to work in that bookstore, and I am planning not to return the phone call, no matter what Mom says.

Chapter Eleven

**THIS IS MY BOOK AND THE CHAPTERS
CAN BE JUST AS LONG I WANT**

Some people would still call this Monday night, but it's
actually very early Tuesday morning and I can't sleep.
Because I can't sleep, I've been rereading this manuscript
and I am quite happy with the number of words I have
written so far: 21,717, to be exact. It makes me feel very
capable to have written this many words, and very lucky
to have the numbers include two sevens. The length
of my chapters bothers me a little because some are
long and some are short. For example, the last one is
extremely short. But since this is my book, I have decided
the chapters can be long or short, and readers will just
have to adjust their expectations as they go along.

I am satisfied with my new laptop and the freedom
it allows me. I can write what I want, even swearing.
I wasn't allowed to swear on the laptop I used in high
school, and I think this jeopardized my rights and

freedoms. People should be able to swear if they want to, even if it's a bad habit, whether they have special needs or not. Swearing is a uniquely human ability and therefore kind of a right, but people have to take the consequences of using inappropriate language, and that is part of being human as well.

My high school English teacher, Mrs. Thomson, said that writing my feelings down can help me understand them. I'm not sure if this is true or not. I have already written about the ways I don't like the bookstore, but what I really need writing to do is help me change these feelings. I know that tomorrow I will have to phone the manager of the bookstore, and I don't feel glad about doing that. But I realize that I am almost nineteen years old and I have a responsibility to return someone's phone call when the person asks me to.

As I am writing this, I count the things I like about the bookstore. The books in it are all brand new, and they have a nice smell. The walls are high, and the building reminds me of a church, and the feeling you get in the middle of a forest with tall trees around you. There is a ladies' washroom in the bookstore. And the floor is shiny.

The truth is that I really do want a job at that bookstore. I am just not sure I can handle it. I wish I could.

I also wish I didn't feel like cleaning things all the

Waiting for No One

time. I've already cleaned the dresser in my room twice today and I know it isn't dusty, but I feel like cleaning it again. Lately, I feel like cleaning a lot of the time.

Something about all this cleaning makes me think of a gerbil, digging in wood shavings that aren't deep enough to make a nest. Because the wood shavings aren't deep enough, the gerbil keeps on digging and digging. My obsessive cleaning doesn't work for its purpose, and no matter what I do, I can't make myself believe things are clean. In fact, the more I clean the more I seem to want to clean.

Now that I've written this, I feel like going to sleep. There is a word for a condition that makes you sleep whenever you are truly anxious, and I think maybe I have it, but only part of the time. I just can't remember what it's called. I wish I could remember because names for things are very important.

And I wish I could learn the tango before I go back to dance class. I also hope doing the tango doesn't hurt my arm, which is supposed to be sore but really isn't.

Chapter Twelve

MY MOTHER'S PROBLEM

When I wake up, I hear sobbing. I listen carefully for a moment, and then feel relieved that it isn't me who's crying. I get out of bed and go down the hall to my mother's room. I open the door and go in, because you don't have to knock if you're worried about someone. She is wrapped in her old pink bathrobe. Her face is all puffy. It looks like it usually looks most mornings, and I'm not sure she is crying until I see the wetness on her cheeks. Then I know.

"What's wrong?" I ask.

"Nothing," she says. "You slept in and you're going to be late for your biology lab."

I look at my atomic watch. It's nine o'clock

"Wow," I say. "I did sleep in!"

She sniffles.

"I think you're crying!" I say. "And why aren't you at work? You always work on Tuesdays."

"I took the day off," she says. "I feel too miserable."

"Do you want me to get you an apple?" I say. "You like apples."

"No," she says, and sighs. Then she kind of laughs and rolls over towards me. "I'll be okay."

"Why are you crying?" I ask, sitting down on the bed beside her.

"I spent the whole Thanksgiving weekend alone," she says.

"That sounds pleasant," I answer. I feel anxious because she is sad, and I take a Kleenex and start scrubbing the dust on her bedside table.

"No, it isn't pleasant. It's lonely and boring," she says. "I thought I might have a date on Saturday, but it didn't work out. And stop with all the cleaning. You are getting pretty obsessive. It's like your switch is stuck on 'super clean'."

"I don't have any switches," I answer.

"It's just figurative," she says, and sighs.

"I am thinking about the germs," I say. Then I wipe her bedstead, which is made of wood from pine trees, and go on talking. "Maybe you pick the wrong kind of men," I tell her. "You always pick men with dark hair and golf shirts who are the same height as you. These are not working out. Why don't you pick someone who likes plates that are all different and never buys matching china?"

She snorts.

"I'm not kidding," I say. "Why don't you pick someone who never had a dog or a cat but maybe had a pen pal?"

"A pen pal?" she asks.

"A pet pig named Snout that eventually died but left a grandchild behind in the pen? Why don't you pick someone who wears jogging suits and who lives in Cody, Wyoming?"

"Taylor, your dad and I haven't been married for years. We're not going to start again now. And as far as I know, he has never owned a pig."

"I was thinking more of Sadie," I say.

"Sadie?" she asks, and her voice sounds like it has a sharp edge to it.

"Dad's girlfriend. Sadie ... uh ... Sadie Hawkins."

"Her name can't be Sadie Hawkins!" Mom cries, and kind of laughs at the same time. "I knew he was seeing someone but I wasn't sure how serious it was. Are they living together? What does she look like?" I ignore the first question because it's rhetorical: they are both living, and I did see them together, obviously.

"She looks like Julia Roberts in that movie we saw ads for on TV," I say.

"Really?" says Mom. Her voice has an even sharper

sound in it now, as if she would like to cut Sadie to pieces. When I look at her, she has the H of wrinkles in the middle of her forehead.

"And her name isn't Sadie Hawkins," I say. "It's Sadie Something Else but I can't remember the Something Else part. Anyways, she is the one who had a pet pig, but I don't mean for you to pick Sadie for a partner because you aren't gay, and she's probably not, either. And she's already taken. What I mean is that you should pick someone like her. Someone who likes plates that are different."

"Thank you, Taylor. I appreciate your advice," says Mom. The way she says this means she isn't appreciative or thankful. Something in her tone tells me to get out of her bedroom and get some breakfast, which I do. I put an apple on the table in case she wants it for later, and then I get ready to go to my biology lab. I ignore the note she has left on the table, telling me to call Mrs. Timmons before I leave. I am afraid to call Mrs. Timmons. That's the truth. Sometimes waiting for something is easier than doing it. Instead, I feed Harold Pinter, give him fresh water, and pet him for thirty seconds. I am not sure if he knows I'm petting him because he is sleeping, but even if it isn't comforting to him, it is comforting to me. He has been sleeping a lot more than he did before we

Beverley Brenna

went to Cody, Wyoming. I think my mother was right. Gerbils should not travel on buses. Maybe he has that sleep disorder where you sleep because you are truly anxious. Before I leave him, I make sure the book called *The Care and Keeping of You* is back on top of his cage. I will never again let him escape. It is my job to protect both his physical and his mental health.

Chapter Thirteen

BIOLOGY LAB

It is Thursday and I am worried about being late for my biology lab. It is a difficult day because it snowed—even though it's only October 17 and it is not supposed to snow until after Halloween. Because of the snow, I can't ride my bike anymore. Plus I think my arm is hurting again from being strained but not broken. Either my arm is hurting or my tooth, and I can't quite tell which. Because I can't ride my bike, I have to adjust to the bus schedule, and that's hard when you have trouble getting used to new things.

Luke Phoenix gets on the bus and I recognize him. He sits in front of me and I ask him if he knows his name is a kind of a bird.

"A luke-bird?" he asks.

"No, a phoenix," I say. "A phoenix is a mythical bird with crimson and gold plumage. At the end of its life cycle, it builds a nest of cinnamon twigs and then sets it on fire,

Beverley Brenna

burning itself to ashes from which a new young phoenix emerges." Then I see that his mouth is curving up and I realize he is teasing. He does know what a phoenix is!

"*Thou wast not born for death, immortal Bird! No hungry generations tread thee down* … John Keats, 1819." Luke Phoenix looks at me. I look out the window and think: one hundred and eighty-three years is a long time. The tires of the bus make a squeaking sound as it carries us through the snow.

In fourteen minutes, we are sitting in the lab and we will be here for three hours. I am lucky that I was not late. There are only eighty of us, and I'm not sure what the other one hundred and forty biology students from my class are doing. Maybe they have their labs at another time. The person who usually sits in the seat beside me is away and Luke Phoenix is in her place. I do not know why he is sitting here. On other days before this one, he sat somewhere else.

We have begun a new unit in biology called Botany. It is the study of plants. Today the lab instructor tells us that flowering plants are called angiosperms, which is a cumbersome name compared to the word *plants*. Angiosperms form seeds in a protective chamber called a plant ovary. These flowering plants can be divided into two groups: monocots and dicots, based on the type of leaves that first appear on the plant embryo.

Luke Phoenix and I are supposed to share a microscope and look at the vascular bundles inside the stem of an orchid, which I have just discovered is a monocot because the embryo of orchids has only one seed leaf. Most angiosperms are not monocots, which I would have guessed because orchids are very rare plants and quite different from other plants.

I am not feeling comfortable. My knees keep bumping against the handles of the drawers at our table. I have drawn my scientific illustration as best I could, including the full taxonomic classification of the orchid in the top corner. Below the drawing, in the middle of the bottom of the page, I have included the magnification calculation, which tells people the distance between the test specimen and the image.

"How did you do that?" asks Luke.

"Yes," I say, not really knowing what he is asking.

"Your drawing is amazing," he says. "How did you learn to draw like that?"

"Yes," I say again, thinking he must be asking a rhetorical question but feeling anxious, nevertheless.

"Sometime you'll have to show some of your work to my dad," Luke says. "He can recognize artistic talent better than I can, but I think you could sell these things."

"Sell them?" I say. "I just want to get 100%."

"Well, you might think about selling them," he replies. "You just might." Then he looks into the microscope to work on his own drawing.

"This isn't as exciting as the fetal pig," he says, staring down through the lens.

"What are you talking about?" I ask.

"After Christmas, we'll get to dissect a fetal pig," he says, and I start to feel sick. I think of Snout, eating from Sadie's china plate with the brown stripe around the edge, except that it's all smashed and Snout is probably dead by now, with his grandson the only pen pal left. Sadie's first husband is dead, too, and I wonder about the number of husbands she had in all. I also wonder, what if people could regenerate like the phoenix and then her first husband would come back and my father would not have a girlfriend. And while I am wondering these things, Luke is saying he can't see the vascular bundle and would I stop bumping the table because it's shaking the microscope. I stand up and I'm not sure what I'm saying, and then I walk out into the hallway to salvage as much as I can of my IQ. Taking deep breaths, I count backwards from ten to one, and then I start worrying about the questions people will ask if they see me out here during class time. Then I start worrying about my assignment, and what if Luke Phoenix is destroying it. Like one time I had a notebook on my desk at school and some other kid who sat nearby took my notebook and started eating the pages. His name was Arnold Fleck and he had a disability—I can't remember which one—that made him want to eat things he wasn't supposed to eat. He wanted to eat inedible items all the time. I am glad I only have Asperger's Syndrome because I have never wanted to eat inappropriate things, but I think pregnant people crave unusual things, so if I am ever pregnant, I might want to eat something like grass from a golf course or Hilroy notebooks. At the same time as being glad I have Asperger's Syndrome and worrying about what I will eat if I get pregnant, I also wish I could be back in class, finishing the lab, instead of out here in the hallway repeatedly counting backwards from ten.

If I can't make myself return to the classroom, I will not pass this class. The more I think about being out of control, the more I am out of control. I end up sitting on the floor at the end of the hallway, with my face pressed into the corner. I am not yelling but my eyes are closed because everything is so bright. I am sitting here, wishing darkness would come gradually and stay forever, and I am hating everything. Most of all, I hate myself.

Beverley Brenna

Our unit exam marks are posted in the hallway beside our student numbers, and after eleven minutes, I feel calmer and stand up to look at them. I got 100%. The test was easy because I could see all the answers in my imagination just as if I had the pages of my notebook in front of me. This visual memory is part of my Asperger's Syndrome and I will try not to look it in the mouth as if it were a gift horse. But having Asperger's Syndrome is also difficult, and right now it is making me wait here in the hallway as if I am waiting for someone, but I am not.

When I finally go back into the room, Luke Phoenix has finished his drawing and is writing his name on his assignment page. He makes all sorts of little curls under it, and I wonder if the lab instructor will mind. He has already told us nine times that lab drawing is not artistic drawing.

"I am glad you did not eat my paper," I say.

"What?" laughs Luke. "Why would I do that?"

I don't answer but sit down and finish my drawing.

"You got the runs?" Luke Phoenix asks. I look at his hands and do not answer. I think he must be referring to my running onto his lawn thirteen days ago, and I do not think he is polite to mention it.

"Do you want me to hand your assignment in, too?" he asks, standing up. I nod, because sometimes you can communicate without speaking, and then I give him my paper. He takes it to the front desk and I look at his pants. They are brown corduroy and kind of baggy. He would look better in jeans, except maybe he doesn't like jeans.

A few other guys around me are wearing jeans, and I see one across the aisle that looks really hot. Shawna and I used to look at some of the guys at my high school and she taught me that "hot" can mean more than just having a temperature over 98.6F. Shawna was a teacher assistant but she didn't help the teachers much. She mostly just helped me. I sent her a postcard last summer and she sent one back from Greece. That's the way I know she is my friend, even if we are not together, looking at guys and deciding which ones are hot. I think this guy wearing jeans in my biology class is almost a ten, except that I am in a university lab with seventy-nine other students and sometime there will be fetal pigs in here. Nobody could really be a ten in here.

I think more about the fetal pigs, and then I take out a spray bottle and clean the top of our table, even though it looked clean to begin with. I feel a bit calmer after doing this and I put the spray bottle away. We move onto the next project, which is an examination of the five major kinds of plant cells: parenchyma cells, collenchyma cells, and schlerenchyma cells, and water-conducting cells and food-conducting cells.

Beverley Brenna

Every now and then, I start feeling anxious and I take out the spray bottle. Using it makes me feel better in the same way swearing works to calm me down. I wonder if using spray bottles works like swearing does to separate us from the animals. I think it probably doesn't.

We are finally finished the lab, and Luke Phoenix goes to hand in the rest of our assignments. I look across the aisle and the guy sitting there is still a nine. When we go out into the hallway, I look at the guy again. Now he is a ten.

Luke Phoenix is reading his unit exam mark and I hear him swearing. I wonder why he is doing that.

"Break, break, break, on thy cold gray stones, O Sea! And I would that my tongue could utter the thoughts that arise in me," mutters Luke Phoenix. "Alfred, Lord Tennyson, 1834."

"One hundred and sixty-eight years is a long time," I say. Luke Phoenix does not answer. He is still looking at his unit exam mark.

"I wish I had done better. How did you do?"

"What?" I ask.

"What mark did you get?" he says.

"I got 100%," I say.

"Maybe you could come over and help me study next time," he says. "I might do better if I work a little harder."

"Or a lot harder," I say, "depending on the percentage

of your mark that you want to improve."

"I should have written down the hard questions after we wrote the exam because the prof said that some of them will be repeated on the Christmas midterm," says Luke Phoenix. "It would be really dumb to answer them wrong a second time."

"I wrote all the questions down," I say. "I remembered them all and added them to my notes. If you like, I could make you a copy."

"You wrote down all the questions? All of them?" he asks.

"Yes," I say.

"Why don't you just come by my place on the way home and I can make a copy there," says Luke Phoenix. "We have a photocopier in my dad's study."

"Okay," I say, and walk out beside him. We take the bus to his house, and he tells me to ask for a transfer so that I can get back on the bus when it's time to go home.

"My car died over Thanksgiving," he says. "I think it's the battery."

In what ways does a car die? They're not like people, I think, but I don't say it. I don't want to sound stupid.

"What kind of car do you have?" I ask instead.

"An old Dodge Neon. It rides like a stoneboat but at least it rides. Usually."

I wonder whether a Neon could possibly be a boat and I'm sure it could not. We go inside his house and right away I can hear his brother wailing.

"It's the monkey," he says, and his mouth makes a grin.

I laugh. I know it isn't a monkey. It's his brother, Martin.

"Hi, Martin!" calls Luke Phoenix. "I'm home and I've brought a friend. Do you want to meet her?"

The wailing stops. I think about what Luke Phoenix just said. Friends are people who do fun things together, and I wouldn't have guessed that he likes looking in microscopes and riding the bus that much.

We go into the kitchen. There is a man there and a boy. The man has on a red apron, and he is trying to feed the boy, who is staring at us. The boy is sitting in a black wheelchair. The man, the boy, and Luke Phoenix all have the same color of hair. It is red and kind of wispy with a little bit of curl.

"Why don't you let him do it?" asks Luke Phoenix. "You treat him like a baby."

"We're in a hurry," says the man. "Martin has an appointment and I don't want to be late."

"You should have started earlier," says Luke Phoenix.

"Hello, I'm Alan Phoenix," says the man, reaching out his hand towards me. I lean over to shake it, and then I realize he is just putting the bowl of mushy food on the counter. I lose my balance and stumble, catching my elbow on the handle of one of the drawers.

"Hello, I'm Taylor Jane Simon," I say, instead of the swear words I am thinking. It is especially unsmart to swear in front of little kids. I look again at the boy and I wonder what age he is.

"May I take your coat?" asks Alan Phoenix.

"Where?" I say.

Luke Phoenix laughs and pulls me back towards the hallway.

"I'll take care of her," he says to his dad. Then he says to me: "You can put your coat in the closet and I'll copy the notes, if that's okay."

"Sure," I say, and get the binder out of my backpack.

"Bye, Martin," he calls, looking back at his brother. "Have fun at your appointment."

Martin closes his mouth but a little bit of food is drooling out. Then he wails again.

After Luke Phoenix copies the notes, we sit at the kitchen table and have banana milkshakes. His father has gone away with Martin, and Luke Phoenix cleans up the table while we talk. I take a cloth and wipe the table near where I am sitting. Doing this makes me feel relaxed and so I do it some more.

"I like your house," I say, because I know this is a

polite statement.

"Thanks," says Luke Phoenix. "We've only lived here a few months. We used to be in an apartment, but my dad finally saved up enough cash for a down payment. People have suddenly discovered his art and he's making the bucks. It's good because he has room here for his studio. Before, he always had to rent a place, which cost even more."

"What grade is your brother in?" I ask after two minutes where we are just silently drinking our milkshakes.

"That's funny," says Luke Phoenix. "Most people just want to know what's wrong with him." But Luke Phoenix is not laughing when he says this. "Martin's in grade seven and he's twelve. He's a pretty cool kid, even if Dad babies him too much."

"Does your mom baby him, too?" I ask.

"No," Luke Phoenix answers.

"That's smart," I say.

"She's not here," Luke Phoenix says.

"That's okay," I say. "Is she in Cody, Wyoming, like my dad?"

"She's dead," says Luke Phoenix. "It was a really hard birth with Martin. His brain was without oxygen for a little while, and that's what damaged the part that controls his body. So he has cerebral palsy. But Mom

113

didn't make it."

"What was your age when that happened?" I ask.

"Seven," he says. "We spent the next year in the States, taking Martin to different hospitals, and I was mostly out of school so I had to repeat my grade."

"I had to repeat a grade as well," I say. "Kindergarten."

"Wow," says Luke Phoenix. "I didn't know anybody could fail kindergarten."

"I didn't fail kindergarten on purpose," I say. "It failed me."

"That's a good way of looking at it," he says. "You were probably too smart for your own good. Or maybe you just put your shoes on the wrong feet."

"No, I always put them on my own feet," I say.

Luke Phoenix laughs when I say this and I wonder why he's laughing. I make my mouth into a smile and take another sip of milkshake. When I am finished, I tell him it is time for me to go, and then I take the bus home. When I get there, my mom is sitting at the kitchen table in her bathrobe and her eyes still look puffy. Some things never change.

"Why are you still wearing your bathrobe?" I ask her. Then I see the calendar and a circle around the number for today, the way we always do when it's someone's birthday. And I remember that it is my brother's birthday, the brother I never actually had because he died before I was born; in fact, he died before he even had a birthday at all. One day, they went into his room where he was sleeping and the angels had taken him. At least, that's what the minister says in church when he talks about somebody who dies, that the angels took his soul up to heaven. My mother is always sad on my brother's birthday. So it's not just that she spent Thanksgiving weekend alone.

"Today Ashton would have been twenty-one," I say.

My mother does not answer.

"Would you like me to get you an apple?" I ask her, but she just shakes her head.

Chapter Fourteen

TEACHING MARTIN TO SWEAR

Today is Tuesday, October 22, and I am over at Luke Phoenix's house and we are hanging out with Martin. Alan Phoenix is finishing some work in his studio and then, he says, we can come in there for a visit and he will show me what he is painting. In return, I am supposed to show him some of my sketches from the lab, and I have brought them in my knapsack. First, though, we are having fun with Martin.

Martin loves experiments. We are making volcanoes by pouring baking soda and vinegar into a mountain we made out of playdough. Martin is using a special machine called a VOCA to tell us what to do next, because he is the leader. VOCA stands for voice-output-communication-aid. It is an interesting machine, with lots of pictures for Martin to press that correspond to spoken words. I have never seen a person use a machine to talk, and Martin is smart at it. In addition to the standard greetings, Luke Phoenix and Alan Phoenix have programmed extra things into the machine that Martin can say.

After twelve minutes, Martin starts banging on the machine and wailing like a brown capuchin. I do not know what he is trying to tell us. Luke Phoenix thinks he wants to say something that he doesn't have words for and that he is mad about that. I look at the volcano. We have poured in too much vinegar and it has run all over, getting the outside of the volcano too mushy to use again. I swear and then I feel badly that I have said words you are not supposed to say in front of kids. Luke Phoenix looks at the volcano and squashes it with his hand. "That's the end of that," he says.

Martin suddenly stops wailing and looks at me. Then he looks at the volcano and kind of nods his head, the tears pouring out of his eyes. Then he begins to shake and move his arms around and scream some more.

"I think he's trying to swear," I say. "Except he doesn't have the words. Instead, he just acts like a primate."

"I don't know," says Luke Phoenix, looking at his brother.

"I'd be even madder if I tried to swear and couldn't," I say. "In fact, I know what that feels like because of the rules about my high school laptop. The teachers wouldn't let me swear on it."

"He's got lots of words he could use if he's mad," says Luke Phoenix. "We put phrases on his VOCA, see?"

Waiting for No One

117

He touches some buttons. "I'm mad," says the machine, in Alan Phoenix's deep voice. "I'm cross. I'm dismayed."

"Those don't sound like words Martin would want to use," I say.

"I'm upset," says the VOCA in its deep voice.

"If I had to press those buttons when my volcano got soggy, I'd be ticked off," I say.

"I am not amused," the VOCA says.

"So maybe that's it," says Luke Phoenix. "That's what he's been trying to tell us! Swear words, but he doesn't have any."

"We shouldn't give him any," I say. "Little kids aren't supposed to swear."

"They're not supposed to act like primates, either," says Luke Phoenix. "And, after all, Martin is twelve—he's not really a little kid anymore."

"Nobody is *supposed* to swear, especially at job interviews," I say.

"Of course, nobody is supposed to swear," says Luke Phoenix. "But people do it anyways. Like our biology prof said, it's part of a cathartic release. Or something. I forget exactly what she said. But why shouldn't Martin be able to swear if the rest of us can?"

"Because swearing is bad," I say. "I wish I didn't do it."

"Would you rather stop yourself from doing it when

Beverley Brenna

it isn't appropriate, or have someone else prevent you from doing it altogether?" asks Luke Phoenix. I look at his red T-shirt and then at his gray corduroy pants. His clothes are stained with lava.

The question he asked is a smart question and I think about it for thirty seconds. I couldn't use my high school laptop for swearing and that wasn't fair. Other kids could swear on their computers, and it would have been reasonable for me to have that capacity and take the consequences if I was inappropriate. Just because I have Asperger's Syndrome doesn't mean I should be cut off from making choices.

"Other people should not be allowed to control my choices," I say.

"Exactly," says Luke Phoenix.

"So maybe we should add some swear words to Martin's VOCA?" I say.

"There's something else I've been thinking about," says Luke Phoenix. "Don't you think it's kind of dumb having my voice and Dad's voice on there, rather than a kid's voice? After all, if Martin could talk, he would sound like a kid, wouldn't he? Not a man or a teenager?"

Martin was rocking his head around, and it looked to me as if he was agreeing.

"Where can we get another kid?" I ask.

"Come on," says Luke Phoenix. "We'll go and see if anyone's outside. Probably they're all inside playing video games, but maybe we'll get lucky." He looks at his brother. "What do you think about this plan?" Martin bangs on his tray and moves his head around.

"He's cool with it," says Luke Phoenix.

We help Martin get on his winter things and then we all go outside. It is very snowy, but someone has cleaned off the front sidewalks and the wheelchair glides along easily. We go all around the neighborhood but there are no kids in sight.

Luke Phoenix goes up to the front door of a green house and rings the bell. There is a little toboggan leaning up against the side of the house. In twenty-one seconds, a lady comes to the door.

"Do you have any kids at home who could help us do something for my little brother?" Luke Phoenix asks.

"What's wrong with him?" asks the lady, just like Luke Phoenix said people do when they first meet Martin.

"Nothing's wrong with him. He just needs a kid to talk into a voice output device," says Luke Phoenix. "You have kids, right? We just live down there on the corner." He points somewhere but I'm not sure where he's pointing.

"Yes, okay, wait here," says the woman, looking down

at the VOCA. In a minute she is back and with her is a girl.

"This is Maggie. She would be happy to help you with the poor little fellow."

Martin starts thumping his arms up and down and making sounds.

"Well, thanks anyways, but we need a boy's voice," says Luke Phoenix. Martin's noises and thumping stop.

"Sorry, only girls here," says the woman. "Come back if you get desperate."

"I can talk like a boy," yells Maggie, trying to make her voice sound deep. "See?"

We turn and go back down the sidewalk. Now Martin is rocking and making more sounds and I think he is choking, but Luke Phoenix says he is laughing.

"Did you think it would be funny to have Maggie's voice coming out of your machine?" Luke Phoenix asks.

Martin keeps on making the laughing sounds. It is starting to get a little dark and I think I should be going home for supper.

Just then a car pulls up in front of another house, and some kids get out. One of them is a boy about Martin's age, and it turns out they go to the same school. His name is Sam and he gets permission to come back to Alan Phoenix's house and talk into the VOCA.

We get him to say all sorts of things, and every now and

then Martin laughs. It's a different kind of laugh, the sounds coming out of him like popping corn, but he's rocking back and forth, and because of that, you know he's laughing. Just before it's time to quit, we get Sam to say some swear words, and then Martin plays them back and we all laugh. We are playing them back for the tenth time when Alan Phoenix walks into the room. He is not laughing.

"What are you doing?" he says, and looks at us. His mouth is in a straight line.

"Martin needed some new words," says Luke Phoenix. "And he needed them in a kid's voice."

"Uh huh," says Alan Phoenix. "It doesn't sound as if the words you are giving him are very appropriate."

"I gotta go," says Sam. "My mom said be back for supper." He runs off to get his coat.

"Aren't you Alicia's son?" calls Alan Phoenix.

"Wooooh, Alicia," says Luke Phoenix. "First name basis."

"Bye," says Sam, and heads out the door.

Something in the way he scampers off makes me think about stories of rats leaving a sinking ship. Shauna told me that sailors know when there's trouble on board because they watch the rats. If the rats run off, trouble is coming. I am guessing that there is going to be trouble in this house. And I am right.

"So tell me more about these words," says Alan

Beverley Brenna

Phoenix. "Do you think it's appropriate for a twelve-year-old to be encouraged to use swear words?"

"Martin's old for twelve," says Luke Phoenix. "He can handle it."

"I'm not talking about Martin," says Alan Phoenix. "I'm talking about Sam. Martin we can deal with. Just by erasing the words. But we can't erase the words so easily from Sam's repertoire."

"We didn't teach them to Sam!" says Luke Phoenix. "He knew those words already. Martin knows them, too, but he just can't say them. How do you think it feels to want to communicate stuff like everybody else when you can't!"

"We're giving Martin every way we can think of to be independent!" says Alan Phoenix, and his voice is definitely in the red zone.

"But he screams like a monkey when he's mad!" says Luke Phoenix.

"And that's not fair!" I yell. "Martin's not a monkey!" My voice is definitely in the red zone. I grab a pillow and use it to rub out the fingerprints on the coffee table. "If I was Martin, I'd want to be able to choose whether to use appropriate words, just like anybody."

There is a silence. Then Alan Phoenix says, "I think you'd better go, Taylor. This is a family discussion and we need our privacy."

There is another silence. It is the silence of a ship that has definitely gone down.

"She can stay," says Luke Phoenix. "She was invited here and I don't want her to go."

I have finished on the fingerprints and now I am rubbing at the arm of my chair with the bottom of my shirt. My switch is definitely turned to *clean* and I can't stop.

"Then I'll go," says Alan Phoenix. "I have to think about this." He gets his coat from the closet and heads outside, the front door slamming behind him.

"Wow," I say.

"Don't worry about it," says Luke Phoenix. "He's always giving himself time-outs."

"Just like my mom!" I say. "She locks herself in her bedroom when she wants to have a meltdown." I am still polishing the chair.

"Dad doesn't have meltdowns," says Luke Phoenix. "He just walks fast."

I think about this for a moment. I'd rather walk fast than have meltdowns. I suddenly have the urge to clean the kitchen, and as I run in there, I wonder about all the fingerprints and which ones might carry germs. I take a deep breath and scrub as hard as I can, but I don't feel much better. Martin cruises in behind me.

"What's your last name, Martin?" I ask.

He presses his communication device.

"Phoenix," it says, in Sam's ten-year-old voice. "I'm. Martin. Phoenix. And you?"

"I'm Taylor Jane Simon," I say. "Are you feeling fine or sad?"

"Like. Shit," Martin says, and then his body rocks in the way that it does when he's laughing.

Luke Phoenix comes in behind him and laughs too, and then he looks serious.

"Maybe Dad's right," he says. "Maybe we shouldn't have given him these words."

"He just has to remember not to use them when it isn't appropriate," I say. "Martin Phoenix, can you do that?"

"Like. Shit. I can," says Martin Phoenix, and his body rocks some more.

"Don't use the bad words in front of Dad!" says Luke Phoenix. "And don't use them at school or you'll get sent to the principal's office!"

"Never. Sent. There," says Martin Phoenix. "Other. Kids. Not. Me."

I decide it's time for me to go home, even though I did not get to see Alan Phoenix's studio or show him my drawings, because I do not want to wait for him to come back. Also, it is time for supper. I go and get my coat. When I look back into the kitchen to say goodbye, I see

Luke Phoenix and Martin Phoenix thumb wrestling. Their hair is exactly the same color of red, and curly in just the same places. It must be nice having someone else with hair that is identical to your own.

"I'm using my dominant hand this time and he's still beating me!" cries Luke Phoenix.

It must be joyful to have a brother. Having a brother means you aren't waiting alone. You can't get a brother back from the angels, so I do not have one. But I wish I did.

Chapter Fifteen

HOW IS A WORD THAT MAKES ME CRAZY

"How could you have done such a thing?" asks my mother, and her voice is in the red zone.

"Yes," I say. That word, *how*, doesn't make any sense, so I try to ignore it and pay attention to the rest of the sentence.

"And don't talk back! I just don't know what you are thinking, to put swear words onto a little boy's computer!"

"It's not a computer," I say. "It's called a VOCA and it represents his speaking vocabulary. Would you like to have an inferior speaking vocabulary? And it's unfair to talk to me and expect me not to answer. Conversations are for two people, Mom!"

She is not listening and on her forehead is the H. I think her IQ is falling fast.

"You have to go back over there and take those words off!" she yells.

"Your voice is in the red zone and I don't have to do

what you say!" I tell her. "You're not the boss of me!"

I told her about helping Martin with his vocabulary because I was trying to explain why I was late for supper. Telling her things is a habit I have to break because more information does not help her feel calmer. If she keeps getting that H on her forehead, I know it is going to stick like that. I go up to my room, and when I come down, I hear her talking on the phone. I listen, because it's not illegal and if someone is talking about you, it's important that you know what they are saying.

She is talking to Alan Phoenix. Alan Phoenix is none of her business because he's Luke Phoenix's father and Luke is my friend. I hear her apologizing, and when she hangs up the phone, I do not want to talk to her because she is making me feel crazy. Except, deep down, I know that I am not crazy; the problem is that my IQ is dropping and it's dangerous to have two people in the same room whose voices are in the red zone. Words are supposed to be the thing that differentiates us from animals. But words are no better than a bark or a howl if you don't know what they mean.

"Swearing allows you to convey your distress!" I say. "I am distressed right now but I am choosing not to swear! This is my right as a person, and Martin Phoenix should have this right just like other kids!"

Beverley Brenna

My mother says some other things but I can't tell what she means, and so I go and lock myself into my bedroom. When the door is locked, I can't slam it and that's very helpful. Because slamming damages the hinges.

Chapter Sixteen

WHAT DO YOU DO WHEN YOUR THOUGHTS GO IN A CIRCLE?

It is Wednesday, October 23, at 11 AM, and I have cleaned everything in my room with a spray bottle and cloth, and now I feel like cleaning it all again. Maybe I do have a switch that's stuck on *clean*, just like my mother said. Under that need to clean, I'm thinking about missing most of Thanksgiving because I was in Wyoming; I'm thinking about Christmas coming out of order, because Thanksgiving is supposed to happen first; I'm thinking about the new professor I will have in my class this afternoon because we are starting a new unit; I'm thinking about going down to the kitchen table where my mother has left a note, telling me I have to call the bookstore's manager before I leave this house, and I'm thinking that I won't ever be able to leave this house because I fully intend not to call the bookstore's manager. And if I don't leave this house, I will not be able to go

Beverley Brenna

to my biology class, and since I do not have a doctor's note, I will probably fail. Which makes me a failure, just what my mother has always been worried about. And failures have to live with their parents forever, a thought that makes my voice want to break the sound barrier. I try counting backwards from ten, and that doesn't help. I count to seven, seven times, and that helps a little. I chew some peppermint gum. I can feel my IQ getting back to normal, but I know it isn't at maximum yet.

I once read the notes my mother took at a conference about autism, and they said that people with Asperger's Syndrome are often very smart but run the risk of not being employable. Eighty-five percent of people with Asperger's do not have jobs. Which means they are not able to live independently. This means their mothers can tell them what to do for dozens of years past the typical stopping point.

I am experiencing a whole cycle of problems related to my cleaning. The problems start with me feeling stressed. Then I worry that I will never be able to function properly in society and live independently. Then I start feeling that the way to calmness is by cleaning things. The more I think about cleaning things, the more relieved I feel when I am actually doing the cleaning, except I am never completely relieved. The more I clean, the less I do other things, and the greater chance I have of not being able to function in society, which means that I will never be independent, a thought that makes me feel stressed, and then I start the whole cycle all over again.

I do not want to be one of the eighty-five percent that is not employable. I know that today the steps I have to follow are: 1. Call the manager of the bookstore, and 2. Go to class. But I can't follow them. My thoughts keep rubbing circles on my brain, just like my cleaning cloth is rubbing the bookshelf. If I am rubbing dust off the bookshelf, I wonder what's coming off my brain, and that makes me worry even more.

Using the spray bottle doesn't make these thoughts stop; I'm still going through Thanksgiving, Christmas, the new prof, the phone call debt, and missing my biology class, and my disappearing brain, over and over in my head. And at the same time, I'm crying and thinking about being a failure and not passing my biology class or ever getting a job, and all the waiting I have been doing and will be doing for the rest of my life.

All the waiting I'll be doing alone.

Chapter Seventeen

THE DARKEST PART OF THE NIGHT

The minister once told us in church that the darkest part of the night is just before dawn. That is a lie. Right now it's Thursday morning at 3 AM and I think the darkest part of the night happened an hour ago. It's still a long time before dawn, because dawn won't happen for five more hours, so the idea that the dark is larger just before dawn is wrong. My own voice inside my head is in the red zone. I am wishing I were sleeping, but I am not, and I am wondering if the part of my brain that controls sleeping got rubbed off yesterday. It is a bad feeling to be awake with loud thoughts when you are supposed to be sleeping. I want to keep cleaning things but my mother removed the spray bottle and, even when I hunted, I couldn't find it. I am lying here, trying to stop my brain from telling me to clean, but the messages to and from my brain are not working properly. It's frightening not to be able to control your own brain.

Last summer at Waskesiu Lake, when I spent the night outside, it was calming not having a roof over my head. I appreciated the quantity of air around me. It's the same feeling I get in church, because the ceiling is so high in the sanctuary that there is a lot of space. I start thinking that maybe if I could go to the church sanctuary right now, I would be able to control my brain.

"What are you doing?" my mother asks in a loud whisper when I start to walk down the stairs.

"I am going down the stairs," I say. "And you don't need to whisper. You're awake and I'm awake and that makes all of us."

I keep going down the stairs and she follows me, and when I start to get on my jacket, she has a meltdown and makes me go back to my room and lie down. By this time, I am crying and trying to tell her that my brain won't stop thinking about cleaning and about wanting to go to church, and she screams that I have to stay in bed and try to relax because it's 3 AM.

"It's not!" I yell. "It's 3:20 AM!"

After the crying and yelling, parts of me start feeling relaxed until, in eleven minutes, all of me is relaxed and I think I can sleep. I don't know what's wrong with my mother, though. I can hear her breathing outside my door. She must be sitting there on the floor in the hallway, and when it's 3:31 AM, that is not where a person should be sitting. I think that maybe my mother is a little bit crazy.

Chapter Eighteen

WHAT I THINK ABOUT WHEN MY HEAD IS UNDER A PILLOW

It's Thursday morning and my mother has made an appointment she didn't tell me about, and it's going to be today. She says she made it in the spring when I was obsessed with the number seven, and that I have been on the waiting list until now, but I think she made it this morning because I heard her talking on the phone. She was talking about when I wouldn't stop cleaning my room with the spray bottle, and she also said that I hadn't gone to my biology class yesterday or made the phone call to the bookstore. I heard her tell the doctor that I have obsessions that are preventing me from leading a normal life. Even though I have my head under my pillow, I can't stop thinking about this. Maybe it's true. When I was looking for sevens all the time, it wasn't so bad. Feeling like cleaning things is worse. It wouldn't be a problem if I were a cleaning lady but I am not. I want to study biology

Beverley Brenna

and work at the bookstore.

While we are waiting to go to the doctor, my mother makes me dial the manager at the bookstore, but the phone transfers to another person who says Mrs. Timmons is away with a bad cold. She should have washed her hands more and kept her desk clean. This is the part about my obsession that is not a problem and I am going to tell it to the doctor. I do not know the doctor's name but I hope it isn't Pain. That was the name of a doctor I heard about once: Dr. Pain. You would think a person would change their name if this was it and they were a doctor.

Although the pillow blocks out my mother telling me it's time to go, it doesn't block out my thoughts. They are louder than ever.

Chapter Nineteen

THE APPOINTMENT WITH THE PSYCHIATRIST

On the way to the doctor's office, I clean the inside of the car, including the dashboard, the glove compartment, and the inside of the passenger door, but my mother does not say, "Thank you." She does not say very much of anything and I can see that the H on her forehead is probably stuck like that now.

The doctor is a psychiatrist and she likes to ask questions. She is asking me things like, "Do you feel your desire to clean things is getting in the way of what you want to do in your life?" and, "If you could reduce the desire to clean things, do you think this would be in your best interests?" While she is speaking to me, I do not look at her face, although I know I am supposed to. Instead, I look at her hands. They are small hands, and she is wearing a gold watch on her left wrist.

"Yes," I say to both questions, and press my thumbs, one after the other, against the inside of my palms. The

Beverley Brenna

doctor talks to me for eight minutes longer, and I like it that her office has a blank wall that I can stare at when I feel like it. After she talks to me, she sends me out into the waiting room, where I use Kleenexes to clean the coffee tables and coat racks while she talks to my mother. Then she calls me back in and the three of us sit together.

"Taylor, I'm going to give you a prescription for some medication to help you with the obsessive thoughts," the doctor says.

I do not answer. She can give me pills but she can't make me take them.

"I'll start you on forty milligrams. If you have any trouble with the medication, such as side effects, please give me a call."

"What are the side effects?" I ask, putting my hand on my side even though I know that's not what the phrase refers to.

"Some people have gotten a dry mouth or a mild sick feeling in their stomach from taking these pills," the doctor responds.

"Oh," I say.

"I will make sure the pharmacist gives you a page about the drug," says the doctor. "Most people say it helps with their symptoms, and the side effects seem to be limited to a dry mouth and maybe nausea or tiredness at the beginning. I will want to hear about anything you notice once you start taking it. Does this sound like an okay plan?"

"I took pills a long time ago, when I was in grade five," I say. "They made me wish I was dead. Pills are not my bag. That means they are not something I care to use."

"I can understand it if you are worried about this," says the doctor. "I have your medical history here and we are trying a newer drug, which I hope will do the job we want without giving you any bad feelings."

"In what way does it do the job?" I ask.

The psychiatrist pauses for a moment. Then she tells me a lot of things about obsessive-compulsive disorder, or OCD, which she thinks I have in addition to Asperger's Syndrome.

"The medication will also help with any feelings associated with depression," she says.

"I am not depressed," I tell her. "But my mother spends a lot of time with puffy eyes, taking days off work and sitting around the house in her bathrobe."

"I do not!" my mother cries.

"You do so," I say. "You look like Lee Marvin, except I do not see you drinking alcohol out of bottles."

"Who is Lee Marvin?" asks the psychiatrist.

"An actor who plays a character in *Cat Ballott*," says

my mother. "And a connection that is not very flattering. Anyways, I'd rather not talk about my problems."

The psychiatrist pushes up her glasses and writes something on a little pad of paper.

"I can talk to your mother another time, Taylor," says the psychiatrist. "This appointment is for you."

"Then why is she in it with me?" I say. "Why does she have to be here, and why does she answer questions for me as if I were a little kid?"

"Your mother cares about you and wants to know the details of your treatment," says the doctor. "But we can keep things more private next time, if you wish."

"I wish," I say.

"So I would like to see you again in four weeks to ask you how you are doing," she says.

"Don't say 'how'; say something else," I say. "Talk so I can understand you, because I have to know what you're saying!"

"Taylor!" cries my mother as if I have done something to hurt her, which I have not, because I am sitting in a chair out of reach.

The doctor looks at me and I see her nodding her head. "You're right, Taylor. I should talk so you can understand me," she says. "What I mean is I need to start you on a dose of medication but I am not sure if it will be the right dose. When you come back in four weeks, I will be able to ask you how you are doing, or you can call me before this and let me know."

"I won't be able to answer!" I say. "I just won't know what you mean even if I do take the pills! I have a gerbil at home and his name is Harold Pinter and he lives in a cage in the basement, instead of under my bed where I really want him, but my mother doesn't think pets belong under your bed. She thinks pets go in the basement and people go upstairs, which is not the same perspective everyone shares. Especially everyone in our house, because I am at least fifty percent, and my perspective is the opposite of hers."

"Taylor, why won't you be able to answer when I ask you that question?" says the doctor, and her voice is so quiet that I realize my voice has been up in the red zone all along and I feel unsmart to have been yelling, and then I feel embarrassed because there is a rule that you're not supposed to yell at doctors.

"I need to go to the bathroom!" I say. "And it better not be an outhouse because I hate those!" I hear my mother and the doctor talking quietly as the receptionist takes me down the hall and unlocks a door. I open it and go inside and, luckily, it is a standard washroom, and I run water on my hands and take a deep breath. I remember what happened in the bus and I quickly open the door, just to make sure that it opens. Luckily, it opens easily, and once I realize I can step out anytime I wish, I close it again and run some more water. My cheeks are hot and I splash water on them and then pat my skin dry with a paper towel. I look in the mirror at what my mother calls my rosy complexion, but no matter what way I stare, I can't see any of the roses on myself. Just little pink dots. I think about artists who make their paintings this way, with little dots. *Pointillism*, it's called. Alan Phoenix makes some of his paintings this way, in the style of an artist called Claude Monet. After he told me this, I looked up Claude Monet on Wikipedia and learned other things. I discovered that Claude Monet died of lung cancer. I bet he smoked.

There is a tap at the door and I hear my mother saying, "Taylor, it's time to come back to the doctor's office."

"Just two more minutes," I say. I finish running the water, and turn it off. I use a paper towel to shine the taps. I carefully dry my hands. Then I open the door. I am ready to go back.

"Taylor, let's begin where we left off," says the doctor. "You were telling me about a question you found difficult."

"I don't want to think about that," I say. "We should talk about something else."

"I won't ask you the question," the doctor says. "But I would like to know what it was."

"How are you doing?" I say in a voice that I know is barely audible.

There is a silence. Then the doctor says, "Fine, thank you."

"No," I say, and I like it that there is another silence. It means that this doctor is listening to me. I take a deep breath.

"The question I don't like is, 'How are you doing?'" I say.

"What is it about that question that you don't like?" asks the doctor slowly. "Is it too personal?"

"That word in it makes me confused," I tell her.

"What word?" she asks. I take a quick look at her chin and then move my gaze up to her eyes. They are green.

"*How*," I tell her.

"You don't know what that word means?" she asks softly. "*How* is the word that bothers you?"

"No," I say. "Yes." I don't know which question to answer first. And then, because I'm feeling embarrassed, I say, "And I don't want to know, either."

She doesn't say anything, and in a minute I feel like talking again. I think I need to make my explanation clearer.

Beverley Brenna

"I won't know what you are asking," I say, taking deep breaths and starting to rub the dust off the coffee table with my sleeve. "You could ask me if I have a sore throat, and I will know. You could ask me if I have been sick to my stomach or dizzy, and I will know that as well. But when you say that other word, it makes me feel as if I am on the edge of the precipice."

"What precipice?" asks the doctor, and her voice is even quieter.

I rub the table hard before I answer.

"The one I'm going to fall into if I hear that word, because it makes me think of nothing without having a harness, and words aren't supposed to do that. Words are not a bark or a howl. Words are supposed to be meaningful."

There are tears on my cheeks and I wipe them away. I don't know if there's a rule that you're not supposed to cry in front of doctors, but I think maybe there is because my mother is standing up. The doctor does not stand up.

"That's very interesting, Taylor," says the doctor. "When you hear this word, it bothers you because you don't know what it means?"

"I just skip over it," I say, and take a big gulp of air. "But it feels confusing to do that. As if you are reading a book that has words snipped out of it and, while you're trying to guess what they mean, the conversation goes on and suddenly you're falling off the cliff."

My mother sits down.

"Have you ever looked this word up in a dictionary?" asks the doctor.

I shake my head. She stands up and goes over to her desk.

"I keep a dictionary here because sometimes I discover words I don't know. Sometimes it helps to look them up."

"I never thought of doing that with this word," I say. "Usually when I hear the word, I start to get confused and then I get mad because of the precipice, and then my IQ goes down and I become too stupid to use a dictionary."

"We'll look it up right now," says the doctor. She brings the book over to me and we look up the word. The first definition for *how* says that it's an adverb, and explains that it means, "in what way."

"So when someone says, 'How are you?'" I say, "they are really asking in what way am I?"

"Yes, and they mean ways like fine, happy, or sad," she says.

"Okay," I say, "and also embarrassed or stupid with a falling IQ."

"That's right," says the doctor. "But there are other ways to use the word *how*, as well. See, right here, it says it can mean, 'for what reason.' For example, 'How could

Beverley Brenna

you have done such a thing?'

"I've heard that before," I say, looking at my mother.

"Then there's kind of a math definition," says the doctor. "*How* could refer to *what extent*, as in, 'How deep is it?'"

"I've heard that before, too," I say. "In my biology class. It was on our exam, but I already know that when you hear a question like, 'How cohesive are the hydrogen bonds between molecules of liquid water?' the answer is, 'They last only a few trillionths of a second, yet, at any instant, many of the molecules are hydrogen-bonded to others, which makes the cohesion of water much stronger than for most other liquids.'"

"Excellent," says the psychiatrist. "I think you are a smart problem-solver, Taylor. Even without knowing some of the words in the exam question, you were able to provide a good answer by memorizing the script, which is, I think, one of your best strategies."

She looks over at my mother.

"We could do some good work if we met on a regular basis," the doctor says.

"Do you teach biology?"

"I try to teach the things people need to learn in order to be able to go out into the world and study biology," says the doctor. "Or whatever else they want to study. Sometimes we get in the way of ourselves, Taylor. Sometimes we just need a little help to get out of our own way and get on with life."

"I don't understand," I say.

"Taylor, the medication I'm prescribing should help you control yourself better. But pills won't solve everything. Talking with me about strategies could help you a lot."

I think about that. What she is saying makes sense. I am aware that people are very complex beings. Even though they are with themselves all the time, they still need to find themselves—at least that's what my dad said. So it makes sense that they could get in their own way.

"I agree with you on one point," I say. "Pills could not solve every problem." Then my mother stands again and I know it is time to go.

"My mother is afraid of words," I say, standing up as well.

"I am not afraid of words!" my mother says.

"You are. You are afraid of swear words."

"I am not afraid of swear words! I just don't care to hear you, or anyone else, use them," she says.

"Will the medication help me make choices about swearing?" I ask the doctor. "Will it help me use appropriate language during job interviews?"

"It should help," says the psychiatrist. I see that she

has a dimple in her left cheek.

"I will let you know," I say. I will not mind coming back here in four weeks because I like her green eyes. They are the same color as a cat's eyes. "And could you please write me a note for my professor, clearing my absence from class?" I ask. "But please don't put OCD in it because that's private."

The doctor nods and says, "Yes," both at the same time. I watch as she reaches for a pad of paper and writes something down.

"What is the name of the condition that makes you sleep when you're truly anxious?" I ask.

"Well, there's post-traumatic hypersomnia," says the psychiatrist. "Why?"

"I think my gerbil has it," I say.

"Please make another appointment with my receptionist on your way out," says the psychiatrist, handing me the note about my absence. I think she is smiling.

"For my gerbil?" I ask, although I really don't think that's what she means.

"Very funny," says the doctor. "For you, Taylor. I look forward to talking with you again."

"We will," says my mother, which makes me mad because the doctor is speaking to me.

"I'd like to see how this medication works," says

the doctor, "and then start some behavioral therapy in the New Year. It's generally quite effective for patients with OCD if we combine medication and other therapy together. We want to get you shipshape as soon as we can, Taylor."

"I'm not going anywhere, and if I do go, I generally take the bus," I say.

Chapter Twenty

WAITING

My mother has told me she can't force me to take the pills, and that I have to make up my own mind. The problem is that my mind is not like a bed. It's not easy to make my mind smooth. All day I have been thinking about taking the pills. My dad called to talk to me but I didn't want to talk to him until I had cleaned the receiver, and then by that time he had hung up, and so I didn't get to talk to him at all.

I know what the doctor meant about getting in my own way. I can see the things I want in life—jobs and university classes and talking to my dad on the telephone—all lined up at the end of the path, and there I am, sitting under a tree, just waiting, in the way of myself and preventing myself from getting by.

But I am afraid to take those pills and so I don't take them today.

And I don't take them on Friday, either.

Chapter Twenty-One

MAKING A DECISION

This morning I go downstairs to talk to Harold Pinter. First I give him clean water and some food pellets, because pet gerbils should always be free from thirst and hunger. Then I take him out of his cage and cradle him on my arm and pat him a lot. He seems to be getting fatter and I can't feel all of his bones the way that I used to.

"The doctor wants me to take pills," I say. "And I hate pills."

He quivers a little bit and I keep petting him.

"I want to be able to go to my biology class and get a job," I continue. "But I want to clean things all the time and it's easier to stay in my room."

Harold Pinter just listens.

"People who stay in their rooms are like Stanley in the play I saw last summer, and they cannot be independent," I say. "At least, they cannot be independent in the way that I want to be independent."

Beverley Brenna

Harold Pinter quivers again and I wonder if he is cold. I put him back down into his cage and he nestles into the wood shavings.

"If you want something to change, there has to be a catalyst," I tell him. "You can't just put the same things together and expect something different to happen."

He looks up at me with his small dark eyes.

"I don't want to be stuck in my room," I tell him. "Waiting for things that never happen."

Harold Pinter keeps looking at me. I take a deep breath. I know what I have to do.

"I'm going to take the pills," I say.

I go up to the kitchen and take the bottle from the top of the refrigerator. I screw off the cap and take out a pill.

"Taylor, are you going to take those pills?" my mother calls from the living room. "You should listen to the doctor, and if you don't, I just don't know what I'm going to do with you."

I get myself a glass of water. Next time I go to the doctor, I will leave my mother in the waiting room. My mother can have her own appointment if she wants. If I see my mother sitting around again in her bathrobe with puffy eyes, I just might make the appointment for her.

"It's my decision," I tell her, and she doesn't say anything else. I wonder why she is not at work, and then I remember. It's Saturday.

Chapter Twenty-Two

TWO KINDS OF TANGO

Luke Phoenix phoned half an hour ago to ask if I was sick, and now he is here with a copy of the notes as well as assignments that I can do at home. He watches while I do the drawings, based on photographs in the textbook instead of microscope slides.

"You are a good artist," he says. "You should show my dad your work."

"Your dad is mad at me," I say. "For putting those words on Martin's VOCA."

"No," Luke Phoenix says. "He's not mad. Well, he kind of was at first. But then he understood that Martin's VOCA had to be the right voice, you know?"

"Do you like it that you and Martin have the same hair?" I ask Luke Phoenix. "Well, not actually the same, but hair that looks the same?"

"I've never thought about it," says Luke Phoenix. "We have the same sense of humor. But Martin's got more

Beverley Brenna

guts than I have. I think about that sometimes, how I could be the one in the wheelchair. I could be the one who can't talk. And yet Martin can actually talk better than a lot of other people. Or maybe he just has more to say. I wonder—I don't know if I could have handled things the way that Martin handles them. *'Do not go gentle into that good night.'* That's a poem by Dylan Thomas, published in 1952, and it's about dying, but it could also be about living. About how we choose to live our lives."

"Fifty years ago," I say.

"Don't just sit back and let things happen to you," he goes on. "Make things happen."

"I am not sure what you are talking about," I say. "But my mother has made banana poppy-seed muffins and she expects us to eat them."

"All of them?" Luke Phoenix asks, looking at the plate.

"Do you mean that people should never give up?" I say carefully, picking up one of the muffins. I am thinking about my pills and hoping they will work for me. Then I pick up a cloth and start cleaning the table. I'm not sure if I'm cleaning because of the obsession or because of the crumbs. My mother's banana poppy-seed muffins are very dry.

"Can you do the tango?" I ask Luke Phoenix.

"No, but maybe I can learn," he says. "They do it on

that television show."

I put on some music but Luke Phoenix laughs, because he says you can't do the tango to classical baroque. He looks through our CD collection and says he should lend us some of his music because ours is too eclectic for dancing. I don't know what eclectic means and he says it means diverse.

"Like orchids," I say. "There are twenty-five or twenty-six different kinds of orchids here in Saskatchewan. I learned that last summer at Waskesiu Lake."

"Oh," he says.

"They can be shaped like buckets, slippers, helmets, and even flying ducks," I go on.

"Uh huh," he says.

"They are very different from other flowers," I add. "And they need a special balance of heredity and environment in order to grow, just like people with autism. But even though I have autism, I am not an orchid. I am just myself."

"I can see that," he says. I think he is smiling, but he might just be trying to get a poppy seed out of one of his teeth.

We look up tango on my computer, because Luke Phoenix says maybe we can get music online. We don't end up with any music because we discover a different tango site. It's a voice-output-communication-aid, like the VOCA Martin Phoenix uses, but much better, and it is named Tango, as well.

A father of a boy with cerebral palsy who lives in New York invented this Tango. He partnered with the same company that makes gaming stations, and the Tango looks a lot like one of these. It even has a built-in digital camera, so you can take pictures and then use them as labels for things you want the machine to say for you. And it has voice morphing, so you can tape-record something and then the machine will say it in whatever way you choose, in a variety of ways, such as woman, man, boy, girl. Just not monkey. I checked.

It costs thousands of dollars, but Luke Phoenix says it would be worth it. He is going to print out some information to take home to his dad. He thinks maybe they can get the government to pay for a Tango for his brother. That makes sense because the government pays for my medication and Martin Phoenix needs technology the way I need pills, except that his technology is to help him talk and do things and my pills are to help me stop myself from talking and doing things I don't want to say and do.

Now that I have started taking the pills, I am not afraid of them. I have had a dry mouth but no nausea and I do not feel tired. I feel a little jumpy, but maybe this is because I am still concerned the pills will make me wish I was dead. Or maybe I feel jumpy because of the muffins. They are putting crumbs all over the couch.

Beverley Brenna

Chapter Twenty-Three

CONFRONTING THE MINISTER

After the church service on Sunday, October 27, when I stand in line to shake hands with the minister, I confront him. I tell him that I know that the darkest hour is not before the dawn.

"Oh?" he asks. "When is it?"

"It kind of depends, I think," I say. "Last week it was just after 2 AM. And then it very slowly got lighter and lighter until the sun rose."

"Ah," he says. "Well, the important thing is that the sun did rise, praise the Lord."

"Of course it rose," I say. "Where else would it go?" Then I think about this and remember that the sun doesn't really move; it's the earth turning around the sun that makes day and night. But by this time, the minister has shifted his position so that he can talk to the next person in line. I go down to the ladies' washroom and wash my hands. I am glad we had a chance to talk so that the minister doesn't tell any more lies about this.

In a couple of weeks, we are going to get to vote whether this minister stays or whether the congregation will hire a new one. I think I am going to vote for a new one.

Chapter Twenty-Four

ANOTHER DANCE CLASS

On Sunday night when I come to dance class, I am not surprised to see that, once again, there are not enough men.

I stand along one wall with the other women, and the men stand along the opposite wall, and then we walk toward each other. As soon as the instructor tells the women to find a partner, I run as fast as I can toward Clifford.

"How are you today?" he asks, and when he talks, I see that his mustache still doesn't move.

"I will be fine as long as we don't have to do the tango," I say. "The tango makes my IQ drop into the double digits."

He nods as if it is the answer he expects, and then he twists his mouth as if he has a toothache.

"It is not my favorite dance, either," he says.

"Do you have a toothache?" I ask.

"No, just something caught between my back teeth," he says. "The wife made steak."

"Were there poppy seeds on it?" I ask. He shakes his head.

First we practice the fox-trot. Slow, slow, quick-quick. I am still smart at it, but Clifford has not improved. He keeps stepping on my feet.

"Stay off my feet," I warn him, but he doesn't listen and keeps doing it.

After a while, we change partners. The instructor says, "Stop," and then the women are asked to move along the line of dance until they find a new partner.

This time I get Ohad for a partner. His left arm is in a cast. The sling looks very white against his dark skin.

"Hello, how do you do?" he says.

"Taylor," I blurt without thinking, just as I have said to him before. He nods.

"What happened to your arm?" I ask.

He just nods.

"I almost broke my arm, too, in Cody, Wyoming," I say.

"Wyoming," he says and rocks a little bit back and forth.

We do not talk for the rest of the dance, and we don't hold hands either because of his cast. This is just the way I like it.

"It was my pleasure," he says, when we are finished dancing.

"You are smart at not stepping on my feet," I say.

Beverley Brenna

I move to my next partner, and I hear Ohad greet a woman who has come to claim him.

"Hello, how do you do?" she asks him.

"Taylor," he says.

I turn to look at him, but he is not looking at me.

"How do you do?" she asks.

"Taylor," he says again, as if he is answering her. Or maybe I heard him wrong; maybe he said something else.

My next partner is Clifford's wife. Her breath is sour, as usual.

"All right?" she asks, holding up her hands.

"Only if you don't breathe out," I say, as I have said before.

"Stop being smart with me," she says. "Let's just get this over with."

"I'd rather be smart than stupid," I said.

I notice that she does not grip me properly.

"You should take charge," I say. "I do not know where you want me to go unless you direct me to move there. 1952. *Do not go gentle into that good night.*" The line from the Dylan Thomas poem comes to me and I think I know what it means: take charge. Don't sit around waiting as if you were in that play by Samuel Beckett! Get up and get going!

"I'm tired of being the man," she says. "I am the man a great deal."

"Get up and get going!" I say.

"What?" She is looking at me and her eyebrows are like brown seagulls on her forehead.

"You should run for the men. That way you will get one," I say. Sometimes people just need a little encouragement.

Soon the dance is over and we change partners again. This time I get another man. He is an extremely short man whose head only comes up to my chest. The instructor tells us we have to practice the tango. We try a few steps. The man's face is very close to what is private on me. I step away.

"I only like the tango that a man invented for his son," I say to him. "I do not like the tango that is a dance. I am going to go to the washroom." I go into the washroom and wash my hands. Then I stay there until the class is over. While I am in there, I use paper towels to clean the sinks. Then I come out to get my coat.

"See you next Sunday," says one of the instructors.

"Maybe," I say. "And maybe not."

Beverley Brenna

Chapter Twenty-Five

THE PHONE CALL

I walk home through the deep snow. It is smart that I am wearing high boots. I feel calm by the time I get home, but I am jumpy as soon as the phone rings. My mother says it is Mrs. Timmons from the bookstore and she wants to speak to me.

"Hello," I say when my mother hands me the phone.

"Hello!" she answers. I feel as if I need to clean the receiver but I manage to ignore the urge. This is a positive sign.

"Hello?" I say again.

"Hello, is that Taylor?" she says.

"Yes," I answer. "This is Taylor Jane Simon."

"This is Mrs. Timmons from the bookstore," she says. "How are you?"

I can feel my heart beating faster. I look at my atomic watch. It is 4:45 PM.

"Fine, thank you," I say. Then I take a deep breath,

thinking about the power I have now over the word that used to confuse me. "How are you?" I ask.

"Fine," she says. "I think we have been playing telephone tag."

"No, we have not," I say. "I don't play games like that."

"I mean we have been leaving each other messages," she says. "I'm glad I've finally gotten hold of you because I want to talk to you about job opportunities."

"Fart," I say, and then I quickly apologize. "Goddamn it, I'm sorry I said that. Both those things."

"Taylor, I have been thinking about your skills and how we could use you in our store."

"Fart," I say again, turning my head away from the receiver and hoping she didn't hear me. Very carefully I pick up a Kleenex from the table and start wiping the parts of the receiver I am not holding. My face feels hot, and if I looked in the mirror, I know I would be very red with the roses. I want to be in control of myself so much. I want to get a job and make money and be independent.

"I've been thinking about a job we need filled right away, and it's a bit of a different job than the one you were applying for. Would you like me to tell you about it?"

"Okay," I say. I take a deep breath and ball the Kleenex up in my hand.

She says it isn't as many hours, but the pay is more than

minimum wage because they can't always find someone to fill the position. Right now it's open. I ask what is it, and she says that it's a book-straightening position that starts at 9 PM, just when the store is closing, and finishes at 11 PM. It's for six days a week. Not Sundays, because the store isn't open on Sundays and so there aren't any shelves out of order. I stop wiping the telephone receiver.

"I'm hired," I say. She thanks me, tells me when I will start, and hangs up. I can't believe I was so anxious all this time, waiting for her call. It was not that difficult talking to her. I will start on Monday. I hope I will be smart at this job. I hope I will be so smart that soon she realizes I can handle more hours and will offer me a daytime job that is not just straightening books. I think the book-straightening job is the worst job they have. Still, I am excited to get my first paycheck there and this will be something to make my résumé longer, which I have heard is a helpful thing. I hope I will soon have another reference instead of Harold Pinter. And it won't be another Mrs. Thomson, thank goodness!

I think back to the job interview and know that I made some mistakes. I knew as soon as I started talking about gerbils that using Harold Pinter as a reference was, just as my mother had said, not a smart idea. Sometimes she isn't right but sometimes she is, and that's the irritating thing about mothers. Because she was right, I know that I will still have to listen to her sometimes, and that makes me feel a bit mad again and feel like swearing, but I'm going to bake cookies instead, which is something better to do with your time.

My mother was wrong, though, when she said that using the blue paper for my résumé wasn't a smart idea. Blue is cooling and calming, according to Sadie, and therefore just what a person needs for a job interview. I am thinking of the color blue right now, as I am trying to plan the days and weeks ahead.

Next Sunday, I will go back to my dance class and do the tango. I discovered this afternoon on the Internet that the steps are slow, slow, slow, quick-quick, slow; that should not be too hard to remember. On Monday, I will go to my biology class and I won't clean the desk before I sit down. At least, I will try not to do this, even if my OCD is telling me to do it. Then I will go to my new job.

The job is a compromise between the job I applied for and not getting any job at all, and I think I am smart to take it. I will be a strong-willed employee and I will make sure those shelves are well organized before I leave. Soon, maybe I will have a chance at another job.

One of these days, I'll go over to Luke Phoenix's house and see his father's studio. And maybe we will hang out more with his little brother. I remember that Luke Phoenix said his dad needs to get out more. I think that about my mother, too, because if she got out more, she would leave me alone. Maybe my mother and Alan Phoenix should get out together. I have never, ever, seen him wear a golf shirt. I think I will tell my mother about this. But right now I'm going to make cookies. They are going to be shortbread.

Afterword

It is three weeks later.

The cookies I made were terrible. I forgot the eggs, just like last time. My mother keeps telling me I should take a cooking class but I don't want to.

Alan Phoenix and my mother have gotten to know each other. They have been on three dates, except my mother says they are just going out for coffee. In the meantime, a number of things have stopped. I have stopped going to dance class because I hate the tango and I also hate the competitive nature of dancing in pairs. Soon the minister will stop coming to our church because a new minister will be starting. I have stopped wondering if I will succeed at my job because I have been working there for three weeks, and I can tell that I am very smart at straightening the books. My mother has stopped asking about why I think Sadie looks like Julia Roberts, and so I can stop trying to think of an answer for her. My father has stopped asking if I will go visit him in Cody, Wyoming, for Christmas, because it is clear that I cannot go because of Harold Pinter. Harold Pinter has stopped being a boy, and has had babies. Seven babies that are almost three weeks old.

The pet store clerk made a mistake when he said Harold Pinter was a boy. Now my pattern of gerbils is boy, girl, girl, boy, girl: Walnut, June, Charlotte, Hammy, and Harold Pinter. I did not think Harold Pinter was a girl but now I know this is true. The babies are in the nest and they did not get there from the angels. Martin Phoenix wants one, and I am going to give him one for Christmas. His friend Sam also wants one. Martin has used his VOCA to tell people about the gerbils, and I appreciate that because I want to make sure we find smart homes for most of them. I hope I will find homes for six of them. I am going to keep one because Harold Pinter is much livelier now that he is not alone in it. Gerbils are social creatures, and it is much healthier for them to have company. I no longer think that Harold Pinter has a sleep disorder. He was just unhappy being a singleton.

Three of the baby gerbils are girls because they have nipple dents on their upper thighs and arm pits; four of the baby gerbils are boys because they have smooth bellies. I am now very careful when I identify a gerbil's gender. I have learned that it is easy to make mistakes. The gerbil I am going to keep is a boy. He is the smallest of all the babies and looks a lot like Harold Pinter.

A few days ago, the babies opened their eyes, and seeing the world has made them agitated. Instead of being calm and sleeping in my hand, they jump away and bolt around their cage. One of them accidentally fell on her head, but luckily she's fine. Now I make sure I take them out cupped in two hands—my left hand underneath, and my right hand on top—and I always hold them over a pillow, just in case. Life is all about smart strategies.

One night, Harold Pinter deserted the babies to chew on a toilet paper tube, and I took the opportunity to clean the cage. I took the little ones out, very carefully, and then scraped all the shavings to one side, scooped them out, and put in fresh bedding. This was a mistake, because Harold Pinter has become quite obsessive about any changes to the cage. When Harold Pinter scampered around and realized things were different, she seemed to quiver in an upset sort of way and then went back to chewing the cardboard tube even more vigorously.

The pups, by this time, were getting cool and needed to be warmed up and fed, but Harold Pinter wasn't interested and kept chewing at the cardboard for no apparent reason. Finally, I got out the kitten replacement milk I'd bought just in case, because that's what it recommended on the Internet, and then I took the pups into a warm place, which was the kitchen. For two hours, I put one drop of milk at a time into their tiny mouths while Harold Pinter went on gnawing very vigorously in the basement. Eventually, I put the babies back into the nest, and after three more hours, Harold Pinter finally nursed them and all was well. I am not cleaning the cage again until they are weaned. Sometimes I think Harold Pinter has autism. But sometimes I don't.

One other thing: we got our marks back from the biology exam. I got 100%. Luke Phoenix got 69%. He is doing better in his other classes, which are not sciences, and I know he wishes he had gotten 100% in biology because he wants to get a scholarship. I told him that if he was anything like a phoenix, he would rise up out of the ashes and try again. He said it was easy for me to say, since I have a photographic memory, and I answered that it is my Asperger's Syndrome that does it.

Luke Phoenix told me a secret. He said Martin Phoenix said some swear words at school and got sent to the principal's office. He said it was his brother's happiest day ever, because he felt just like the other boys. He also said that his brother has been using the VOCA a little more, and not just for swearing. In fact, not for swearing at all except in very special circumstances, and then he uses it instead of screaming.

I hope that my mother and Alan Phoenix will get married because it would be pleasant to have two brothers with red hair that curls at the edges. However, I have decided that waiting is not the way I wish to spend my life. I have been waiting to finish high school, waiting to take a university class, and waiting to get a job, and now I have done these things. I could be waiting for Christmas, and waiting to turn nineteen, but after that, there would just be other things to wait for, and I am thinking that I will try to just experience these things instead of waiting for them. I know that life does not always go according to plan, but I have promised myself to give it my best effort. I hope I can keep this promise and stay out of my own way.

There is only one thing I am waiting for and that is to get rid of this job straightening books. I do not like a job that is only two hours a day, but Mrs. Timmons says to wait until they have something else come available. I will continue to do my best. I wish I knew a shaman who could give me the power to control things.

One comforting thought is that Harold Pinter and I will be together, very likely until I am twenty-two and Harold Pinter dies, and then quite possibly I will get

Beverley Brenna

another gerbil, and another after that and another after that, because even though you can't always make your family the size you want, or get full-time jobs right away, or live away from the home in which your mother constantly distributes her advice, you do have some flexibility with gerbils.

Interview

WITH BEVERLEY BRENNA

Taylor Jane Simon is a fascinating and sometimes witty character. What made you want to tell her story, in this book and its predecessor, _Wild Orchid_? Why is it an important story to tell?

When I first began crafting the character of Taylor Jane, she seemed a lot like me as a teenager. The more I explored her unique traits, the more she began to evolve as her own person, and the more interesting she became. What I think makes this character work is that she is a combination of real life and fiction, just as good, well-rounded characters should be. I did not have Asperger's Syndrome, as Taylor does, but I did struggle to fill my summers at Waskesiu Lake, and I did want the same independence from my parents that I think Taylor seeks.

As I was developing Taylor as a young woman with high functioning autism, I began to think about how few books present characters with disabilities and how important it is that books mirror real life. Realizing that helped me make the decision for Taylor to have a known diagnosis of Asperger's Syndrome. For so long, writers—especially writers for children—were only writing about a few characters, just dressing them up in different ways but not really changing much. Now we have more diversity available in our reading material, although I think writers still have a long way to go in presenting people with disabilities as capable protagonists who grow and change during the course of a story.

I had not originally intended to write a sequel to *Wild Orchid*, but after the book had been written, I began to wonder what Taylor would do after she returned to Saskatoon. Would she get a job in a bookstore, as she anticipated? Would she conquer her fear of the unknown and register at university? These and other questions worked at me for about a year before I finally gave in and listened to Taylor's voice, telling me what happened next. Even then, I didn't start right in on another novel. I wrote a short story, thinking that would suffice. But when "Something To Hang On To" had been published in my anthology of the same name (Thistledown Press, 2009), I still wasn't satisfied until I had finished the second novel. Now I am at work on a third. It will begin where *Waiting*

Beverley Brenna

for No One leaves off, and then circle back to Taylor's childhood, giving shape to the experiences of bullying that she endured in elementary school.

Taylor has to find a way to fit into a world from which she sometimes feels estranged. In what way do you think her feelings and experiences can be understood by readers who aren't dealing with Asperger's Syndrome?

Part of being human is that we all feel, from time to time, as if we're the "only one." We all feel rejected by others, or embarrassed by our own inability to fit in. This is a universal experience, especially during transition times such as adolescence. This is not to downplay the extreme challenges Taylor has in understanding the world around her, or the difficult time she has in dealing with the unpredictable. Taylor may invoke empathy from readers because she presents feelings with which we all, at times, can identify, although she also offers her own unique experiences of life, which I think are very interesting to consider.

Why did you name Taylor's gerbil Harold Pinter?

Taylor gave her gerbil that name because of her strong connection to Harold Pinter's existentialist plays, especially *The Birthday Party* which she experienced a number of times as a stage play in *Wild Orchid*. Because Taylor is attached to using people's full names, rather than just a first or a last name, she could not comfortably shorten the gerbil's name to either "Harold" or "Pinter"—it had to be the whole thing.

You enjoy writing about young people who are facing unusual challenges in life. Why is that?

Part of my outlook on life is that everyone has interesting stories to tell, and I am especially intrigued by stories I have not heard before. Taylor's story, for example, is one that I had never before encountered in fiction, although I recognized parts of her journey with Asperger's Syndrome from my work teaching students with special needs. The research I did to make sure Taylor presented a realistic picture of Asperger's Syndrome was fascinating, and she taught me so much that has helped me understand some of my students in a more sensitive manner.

Beverley Brenna

Why did you choose to tell this story in first person?

I was intrigued at the connection I initially made between myself as a teenager, and this fictional character that was emerging, a fictional character with autism. I hoped to be able to see the story through Taylor's eyes as a way of trying to live her story, just as an actress might temporarily "become" a person in a play. I thought that by telling the story in this way, it would offer more details and insight to what is going on "behind the eyes" of this complex character who, from the outside, might be described in a narrower way as quirky or incomprehensible.

It wasn't easy to find the right title for this novel, but the one you finally chose has a lot of resonance. Why do you think *Waiting for No One* is so appropriate?

The references that support the title *Waiting for No One* appear as Taylor muses about the different kinds of waiting she has been doing—waiting for a prospective employer to call, waiting to turn nineteen, waiting for all sorts of things that are out of her control. She thinks about the characters waiting for "Godot" in Beckett's play, and realizes that she does not want to be waiting endlessly for something or someone that possibly isn't going to materialize. Taylor thus saves herself from the fate of the characters in *Waiting for Godot* through her own integrity. She decides that instead of waiting, she is going to experience life; this is one of the reasons why she addresses her obsessive-compulsive behavior. She realizes that it has become an impediment to her success. The title *Waiting for No One* really encapsulates the quality of independence that I think drives Taylor's character.

The title also has another, less obvious, connotation. Taylor wishes that in her quest for a boyfriend she could just move along the line of dance and another partner would appear, and yet life is not a dance class. In life she feels that she is waiting for no one—that there may be no one out there for her romantically. This gives the title *Waiting for No One* the potential to also capture the sadness Taylor feels within a loneliness that is part of who she is.

Your published work includes writing in many different genres: poetry for adults and children, short stories, picture books, novels, and academic work. Which kind of writing do you find most fulfilling?

At any given time, the writing that I find most fulfilling is the writing that I think people are reading. Writing is a way for me to connect with others, and so when I am doing school visits, for example, and young people offer ideas and suggestions as well as comments about my work, I really pay attention. I find the transaction between reader, writer, and text to be tremendously motivating.

What advice do you have for young writers?

Keep writing! The more you work at it, the better you become. And keep reading! I'm still learning new ways to craft my work from reading literature produced by others; some of my best learning as a writer has occurred from trying to figure out how another author developed a character, or created a setting, or advanced a plot.

In addition to reading and writing, find someone else with whom to share your writing. If you have a friend who likes to write, get together once in a while to read each other's work, and tell each other what you liked and what perhaps wasn't very clear. This also trains you to be a better editor of your own writing. Often good readers, in particular, do not make good editors of their own work because they are fluently reading along and predicting what would make sense rather than seeing what actually is there, in print. We have to learn a different kind of reading in order to be good editors. I often read my work out loud because this technique slows me down and makes me consider just what I have said. I certainly catch more mistakes when I read a passage aloud, although my dog doesn't like it—and when I put lots of expression into my voice, he whines and tries to drown me out!

Acknowledgements

Quotations from Samuel Beckett's play are gratefully appreciated with the following statement: *Waiting for Godot* by Samuel Beckett, copyright 1954 by Grove Press, Inc. Copyright renewed by Samuel Beckett. Used by permission of Grove/Atlantic, Inc.

Thank you to Steven Pinker for his thought-provoking discussion in *The Stuff of Thought: Language as a Window into Human Nature* (New York: Viking, 2007), including the hypothesis that cathartic swearing is the result of cross-wiring between the mammalian rage circuit and human concepts and language. Rather than a defensive scream as a "response cry," according to Pinker, we are conditioned to use particular conventional language. Gratitude also to Temple Grandin for her inspiring books: *Animals in Translation: Using the Mysteries of Autism to Decode Animal Behavior* (New York: Scribner, 2005) and *Animals Make Us Human: Creating the Best Life for*

Animals (New York: Houghton Mifflin Harcourt, 2009).

Thanks to Dionne Jones for her impeccable Biology 120.3 notes, and Ross Nicholson for his perceptive answers to my questions about being a biology course instructor. The biology textbook Taylor refers to in the novel is *Biology: Concepts and Connections*, Fifth Edition, by Neil A. Campbell et al (San Francisco: Pearson, 2006). Thanks, as well, to Eugene Jeanson for sharing inspiring stories about kids and communication.

Luke Phoenix takes his poetry quotes from *The Norton Anthology of English Literature*, 3rd Edition, edited by M.H. Abrams (New York: W.W. Norton & Company, 1975).

Sincere appreciation to the Saskatchewan Arts Board for their financial support of this project, the Mint Agency for their business savvy, and to my editor, Peter Carver: you are the best!

Kind regards to Thistledown Press for allowing me to recycle here my short story, "Something to Hang On To," from my collection of young-adult short stories, also entitled *Something to Hang On To*.

Thanks to Elaine Domier, The Travel Lady, for her helpful information that came just in time.

Thanks also to Gail Sajtos for her wisdom in helping me further develop the character of Taylor Jane, and appreciation to Tara Goodwin for information about

Beverley Brenna

the Tango. Also, thanks to Shannon Friesen, Executive Director of Autism Services, for her supportive comments. Gracias to my writing club gals: Brenda Baker and Leona Theis, for your enthusiastic guidance. Much appreciation to Joyce Bainbridge, my other mentors at the U of A, and the Starfish Team. Gratitude also to my wonderful family: Dwayne, Wilson, Eric, and Connor, as well as Joyce, Jack, Linda, my cousin Beth, my mother, and my mother-in-law, and the rest of my extended family for your steadfast love and encouragement.

Waiting for No One